Praise for
Kristine Kathryn Rusch

"Kristine Kathryn Rusch is one of the best writers in the field."

—*SFRevu*

"[Rusch's] writing style is simple but elegant, and her characterization excellent."

—Mark Morris
Beyond

"Like early Ray Bradbury, Rusch has the ability to switch on a universal dark."

—The London *Times*

"Kristine Kathryn Rusch's crime stories are exceptional, both in plot and in style."

—Ed Gorman
Mystery Scene Magazines

"[Rusch's] short fiction is golden."

—*The Kansas City Star*

Praise for the Retrieval Artist series

"If you love puzzle mysteries, crime novels, well-invented sci-fi worlds, or stories about characters you can believe in and care about, you owe it to yourself to give Rusch's Retrieval Artist novels a try."

—Orson Scott Card
New York Times bestselling author

"What links [Miles Flint] to his most memorable literary ancestors is his hard-won ability to perceive the complex nature of morality and live with the burden of his own inevitable failure."

—Locus

Praise for the Smokey Dalton series
(writing as Kris Nelscott)

"Nelscott's series setting, in the turbulent late '60s, gives her books layers of issues of racism, class, and war, all of which still seem to remain sadly timely today."

—Oregonian

"Nelscott has her own, very distinct voice, and her series creates its own deeply satisfying pleasures and cogent points."

—Seattle Times

"It's not hard to draw parallels between Nelscott's PI Smokey Dalton and Walter Mosley's Easy Rawlins, another secretive, canny black man trying to solve mysteries while circumspectly navigating the white world. But Dalton's no knock-off. (Would you label the hundreds of hard-boiled detectives who've appeared in Raymond Chandler's wake mere Marlow Xeroxes because they're white?)"

—Entertainment Weekly

Also by
Kristine Kathryn Rusch

The Retrieval Artist Series:

The Disappeared
Extremes
Consequences
Buried Deep
Paloma
Recovery Man
Duplicate Effort
Anniversary Day
Blowback

The Smokey Dalton Series (as Kris Nelscott):

A Dangerous Road
Smoke-Filled Rooms
Thin Walls
Stone Cribs
War at Home
Days of Rage

SILENT NIGHT
A CHRISTMAS COLLECTION
KRISTINE KATHRYN RUSCH

WMG
Publishing

Silent Night

"Boz" by Kristine Kathryn Rusch was first published on the SciFi.com website, December 23, 2005.

"Doubting Thomas" by Kristine Kathryn Rusch was first published in *Villains Victorious*, edited by Martin H. Greenberg and John Helfers, Daw Books, 2001.

"Rehabilitation" by Kristine Kathryn Rusch was first published in *Ellery Queen's Mystery Magazine*, January, 2000.

"The Moorhead House" by Kristine Kathryn Rusch first published in *Ellery Queen's Mystery Magazine*, January, 2008.

"Nutball Season" by Kristine Kathryn Rusch was first published on the SciFi.com website, December 24, 2003.

"Loop" by Kristine Kathryn Rusch was first published in *VB Tech Journal*, November, 1995.

"Substitutions" by Kristine Kathryn Rusch was first published in *Places to Be, People to Kill*, edited by Martin H. Greenberg and Brittiany A. Koren, Daw Books, 2007.

"Snow Angels" by Kristine Kathryn Rusch was first published in *Alfred Hitchcock's Mystery Magazine*, January/February 2006.

"The Taste of Miracles" by Kristine Kathryn Rusch was first published in *Analog*, January/February, 2007.

"Stille Nacht" by Kristine Kathryn Rusch was first published in *Grit*, December, 2004.

WMG Publishing
www.wmgpublishing.com

Contents

SILENT NIGHT

A CHRISTMAS COLLECTION

KRISTINE KATHRYN RUSCH

Introduction

WHEN I MET DEAN WESLEY SMITH, the man who would become my husband, neither of us had any money. It was 1986 and we were both struggling writers. I was a working nonfiction writer, and Dean had published quite a few short stories. He made his money as a bartender. I gave up nonfiction to try my hand at fiction and got a part-time job as the world's worst secretary. (The ad didn't ask for the world's worst secretary; I just ended up with the title.)

As the holiday season approached, we tried to figure out how to be festive while broke. We had a lot of writer friends who also had no money, except for the handful who had Real Jobs. So we wanted an equitable division of presents. We didn't want one person to spend five times the funds that someone else did, even if the first person could afford it. We both knew from personal experience that such differences in gift giving felt awkward at best.

The first Christmas we didn't give any gifts. But the next year, we figured out what we wanted. We wanted a festive, writerly Christmas. So we invited a group of our writer friends. We had turkey and pie and cookies and all kinds of yummy treats. We had to buy gifts for everyone who came but—and here was the catch—we couldn't spend more than one dollar per person.

And then, when the feasting and the gift giving ended, we sat around the fire (or a makeshift fire, if no one had a fireplace) and read Christmas ghost stories to each other, ghost stories we had written.

Some years, the stories were horribly gruesome. Some years, the stories were amazingly sweet. One year, Kevin J. Anderson wrote a tremendous Christmas story about Charles Dickens (which he later sold), but the room was so hot as he read that Dean fell asleep. And snored. Kevin, being Kevin, read blithely on, while various people around the room tried (and failed) to wake Dean up.

Eventually, people got married and developed their own family Christmases. Dean and I moved to the Oregon Coast, so the drive back to Eugene, Oregon (where the festivities were held) was simply too burdensome to do in one day. (We made that decision after driving back in freezing fog one Christmas Eve—and we were the only people on the road.)

The holiday tradition continues in Eugene, but Dean and I are no longer part of it. We have our own tradition with our friends here on the Coast, writers and non-writers. We no longer read Christmas ghost stories to each other. But every year, I try to write a Christmas story anyway.

Four of the stories in this volume were written for those Christmas Eve ceremonies, although not a one of them has a proper ghost. "Loop" is a science fiction story in which a woman appears ghostly. And "Stille Nacht" is haunted by the ghost of my mother, who was dying as I wrote the story.

The others were written because I got into the habit of writing something Christmasy for the holiday season. Sometimes the stories only have a whisper of Christmas about them. Sometimes they're just set at Christmas time. Some are sweet and saccharine. Some are bloody and violent. I guess, for me, the season can encompass all of those things.

I don't have quite enough stories to do a big Christmas collection every year, but I'll do one whenever I have at least ten stories to share. So this is the first: The Christmas 2010 collection. You'll find something to fit your mood here, no matter what your mood may be.

Enjoy the collection, and enjoy the season. I do find it magical and I hope you do as well.

—Kristine Kathryn Rusch
Lincoln City, Oregon
November 28, 2010

Boz

BOZ WOKE UP SLOWLY, convinced he was hearing an ancient crooner sing "White Christmas." He pulled his pillow over his head to drown out the noise before he remembered where he was.

Space. The ship. Light years from anything.

Christmas carols? He'd never expected to hallucinate them.

He sat up. His room was filling slowly with light. The on-board systems had been set up to mimic a typical Earth day (as if a typical Earth day had constant sunshine), and they did adjust for the seasons.

When the *Beautiful Dreamer* had been in the planning stages, the crew decided two things: that they'd remain on a 24-hour day, and they'd follow the western calendar. He didn't mind the 24-hour day, but he saw no reason to keep the calendar. He had voted against it and had been out ruled, which was funny, given that he was going to be the only one awake to "enjoy" that calendar.

He sighed, rolled over, and pulled the pillow off his head. Sure enough, some 20th century icon was singing about Christmas. Only the song had changed to "I'll Be Home for Christmas." That was a cruel joke. No one on this ship was going home again.

Not that Boz cared. He hadn't had a home in decades.

He sat up, rubbed his hand through his scraggly hair, and asked, "Computer, what's the date?"

The computer answered in its relentlessly cheerful voice, "December 25."

Christmas.

"I'll be go to hell," he whispered, and then shivered.

The music wasn't playing in the computer speakers. If it was, he would have heard it directly in his room. Instead, it sounded far away, as if someone were playing tunes down the hall.

(It actually sounded just like it used to when he lived alone in New York: Christmas music would waft at him from everywhere—his neighbor's apartment, the nearby storefronts, the street below. He shivered again, not liking that memory. Those days before he'd joined the mission had been difficult ones.)

"Make the music stop," he said.

"I do not register any music." When the damn thing was being negative, the voice grated all the more.

"Well, somebody's playing some, and there's just you and me on this ship." He slipped on clothes, something he promised himself he would do no matter what, because he *was* working, even if the circumstances were odd.

"Correction," the computer said. "There are 656 individuals on this ship. *I* am not an individual. I am a construct designed to…"

"I *know*." He wished he hadn't spoken aloud. He sighed and tried again. "Has someone awakened accidentally?"

"All of the sleep chambers are functioning properly. The crew is unchanged."

"Then where is the music coming from?" Boz asked.

"I do not register any music. Hearing things is a warning sign. Should I call up the holographic psychiatrist?"

"No," Boz said, and decided to stop talking to the computer. If the computer determined he was crazy, the damn thing would wake someone else up—with no hope of that person returning to cold sleep. Then Boz would be stuck with another person—a person who had been told he was ill, injured or had mental problems.

He couldn't cope with that.

The music had changed again. Now young people's voices rose in "Happy, Happy Holiday Time." At least that tune was a little more modern. The chorus of pure children's voices gave him a sudden longing for snow, of all things.

Snow and chill air and a breeze. What he wouldn't give for a breeze.

He stopped just inside his door, and leaned his head on the metal. He hadn't had this kind of homesickness since the first month. He'd been alone on this vessel for nearly a year, and for the most part, it hadn't bothered him, just like predicted.

He was an off-the-charts introvert, someone who would live alone even if he were given the choice to live with people he liked, someone who preferred his own company to everyone else's—at least, that was what all the battery of tests said. The tests had been strictly anonymous—done by number, so that the researchers wouldn't look at the subject's history. Once his number was revealed, all Boz's personal history did was confirm the diagnosis.

No marriages, no children, his parents long dead. Boz had lived alone since he was sixteen years old, and hadn't missed the company.

But the point wasn't ancient history. The point was Christmas carols—"Jingle Bells" now (what did that song mean, anyway?)—and the fact that the computer denied any knowledge of the sound.

Something had malfunctioned, oddly malfunctioned. He would find it.

He pulled open the door. The music got louder. He could hear piano and drums behind those children's voices, singing happily about dashing through snow (ooh, the longing *again*: he shook it off. He couldn't get lost in nostalgia—he had two more years of breezeless-ness ahead). The smell of hot cocoa warmed him, and made him think of the only Christmases he'd ever celebrated: those with his parents.

Hot cocoa?

He looked down. A tray sat just to the left of his door. A mug with something that looked like hot cocoa and steamed like hot cocoa sat on one edge of the tray. In the center, a coffee cake glistened, the frosting so fresh it slid off the side.

His stomach growled.

He bent down, and touched the tray. It was real. Had he ordered it? The three 'bots that had been brought along to make his life easier would put a tray out if he wanted it. He had never wanted one before.

He touched the mug, recognizing it as one of the ship's set. He only used his personal dishes, an affectation the captain called it, but part of the ritualized necessities that kept him going.

The shrinks had said that he wasn't mentally healthy— at least when it came to socializing—but he was exactly the kind of person to be left alone on the ship for the three years it took to get to the new colony. Initially, colony vessels like the *Dreamer* kept three or four people awake to handle back-up problems, but the monotony put them at each other's throats. More than one "accidental" death had changed that policy, and then the shrinks got involved.

Competent introverts were the answer.

Boz's problems faced him on the other end, when the ship reached the new planet's orbit, and he woke up the main crew. From then on, he would be in close contact with people, maybe for a year or more.

He worried about it, even now. He had actually told Captain McNeil that the required socializing disqualified him. Boz wouldn't be able to tolerate the living conditions, not just on the ship, but in the colony itself.

"We know," the captain said. Her pretty blue eyes twinkled. He'd often wondered how such a cheerful person had risen so far in the colony programs. "We have several solutions on the docket for you. You can study them as you travel."

His stomach clenched. He didn't want to think about the future. It scared him more than he wanted to admit.

Almost as much as the Christmas carols and the hot cocoa. He crouched, touched the mug, felt the warmth through the unbreakable synth ceramic. Then he stuck a finger in the liquid—very hot—and brought it to his lips.

Hot cocoa. He hadn't had that in years, hadn't thought to make it here either, even though the ship's stores had everything he could ever want.

Then he touched the coffee cake. It was warm too. He broke off a piece. It felt fresh baked.

He took a bite. It tasted like the pastries he used to get in New York, before he moved to Houston to begin training for the colony program. Rich, warm, delicately spiced. A taste of the past, one he hadn't even realized he missed.

The entire morning was unnerving him. Was this some kind of test? If so, who had derived it, and why do it now, when the ship was in flight? They couldn't turn back, and Captain McNeil had explained to him that they didn't want anyone else to wake up if at all possible.

He ate the coffee cake, sipped from the cocoa, but left it on the tray. Too much sweetness for him this early in the day. He pushed the tray aside—something to deal with later—and headed down the hall, toward the music.

Instrumental now. Something from the *Nutcracker Suite*. He'd never bothered to learn much about that thing—what he knew about most of the Christmas traditions, he'd picked up as part of the culture. In fact, he'd felt a little relieved to be away from the annual holiday-assault fest.

Christmas.

He hadn't even known.

The music grew louder as he reached the rec room. One of the bots stood outside, a tray of cookies on its head. Christmas cookies, with frosting and sprinkles, and happy holidays written in red and green across the tray itself.

"I didn't program you for this," Boz said to it.

"That is correct," it said in its mechanized little voice.

He let out a small sigh of relief. He had been starting to doubt his own memory.

"Then what's this all about?" he asked.

"You must enter the recreation room," it said.

"First, tell me what's going on," he said.

"You must enter the recreation room," it repeated. "Or have a cookie."

He flatted his palm against the door lock, then grabbed a cookie despite his best efforts not to, and stepped into the recreation room. The music was louder here. The entire place smelled like pine needles. He took a deep breath of the nearly forgotten odor.

In the corner, a tree leaned against the wall. The tree was decorated with tiny multicolored lights, and silver balls that reflected those lights. Beneath the tree, hundreds of presents glistened.

Garland hung around the room, and more lights hung from the ceiling. Their colors reflected on silver disks that lined the floor.

He took a step forward, and one of the disks shimmered. Then a hologram of Captain McNeil rose in front of him. The hologram was cheaply made—Boz could see through her to the tree—and winked in and out, as if it couldn't quite sustain the image.

"Merry Christmas, Boz," she said. The image paused. He sighed. It expected a response.

"Merry Christmas," he said.

She smiled. "I hope you don't mind the intrusion into your routine. We programmed this celebration before we left. We've used your file to design the best holiday we can for you."

The image paused again. He wasn't sure how to respond. Say thank you? For scaring him half to death? He couldn't say that. He couldn't say much of anything. He felt as tongue-tied as he would have if she were actually standing in front of him.

Finally, he managed, "Okay."

"We weren't sure about the music. We programmed our favorites. You can change that program now. The bots will prepare a roast turkey dinner for you with all the trimmings. You're welcome to have it whenever you like."

Her eyes twinkled, even in the damn hologram.

"But do open the presents. Each member of the colonizing team brought something they thought you'd appreciate, something you could watch or read or study in the long years ahead."

His mouth was dry. They gave him presents? Why?

"We wanted to tell you how much we appreciate you guarding our ship for the next few years," Captain McNeil's hologram was saying. "We know you wouldn't be able to take the thanks personally, and thanks means so much less when the task is actually completed. So we thought we'd say it now."

The other disks sprang to life. All 656 colonists stood before him, most miniaturized so that they could fit into the room. He took a step backwards.

Six-hundred-and-fifty-six people staring him—or the image of them staring at him—made him want to flee.

"Thank you, Boz!" they said in unison. "Merry Christmas."

And then, mercifully, they all vanished.

Even the captain.

He swallowed against his dry throat. The music changed—a chorus of out-of-tune voices lustily sang, "We Wish You a Merry Christmas." He had a hunch he was listening to the crew.

The door swished open behind him, and one of the bots entered, a tray of beverages on its round head.

"Mulled cider," it said. "Or coffee or spiced tea…?"

No matter how hard it tried, it didn't sound like a waiter. Boz smiled, in spite of himself.

He took the mulled cider, then sat on one of the couches, his heart still beating rapidly. He reached over and touched the tree. His fingers passed through the branches. Another hologram, only a better one than the disks that scattered on the floor.

Then he reached for a present, expecting his fingers to pass through them. But the box was real. He picked it up. His name was scrawled on it in an unfamiliar hand. The tag said the gift was from someone named Betsy Wilson.

He didn't remember a Betsy Wilson. He felt vaguely embarrassed about that. He picked up the gift, opened it, found a dedicated reader—something with a permanent battery and a voice-over function. He would no longer have to use the computer for his late-night reading.

Thoughtful. Bought with him in mind.

He understood what was going on. This was part of the program to ease him into the colony, to prepare him for the future.

He should probably resent it. Perhaps he should act cynically and say there was no warmth behind this gift.

But there was. The colonists could have integrated him in a thousand ways—he'd read about half of those ways on the first part of the journey (and hoped he wouldn't have to do them). This—this was heartfelt.

He sat on the couch for a long time, clutching his reader, sipping his mulled cider, taking cookies from the tray on top of the bot's head.

Then he made a decision.

The captain was right: Thank-yous after the fact didn't mean as much. He called up the computer log, and had the computer record the room. He hoped the recording would get his face, the absolute awe he felt. Because he wasn't good with words, especially words others would eventually hear.

But even he could say thank you.

And he did.

Doubting Thomas

TOMMY ULRICK DISCOVERED THE SCAM when he was six. He remembered everything about the night clearly: the winter dampness in the air, the smell of wood smoke mixed with ocean, waking on his flannel sheets with an urgency that seemed only to happen in childhood. He slipped out of bed and hurried to the bathroom—one of those herky-jerky emergencies where he jiggled all the way, holding himself, and praying he'd arrive on time.

Which he did, just barely. He remembered the relief, and as the relief grew, so did his chill. Someone had left the large bathroom window open, letting the December cold inside, allowing people on the street below to see his most private moment.

He glanced out—still too compromised to pull the window closed—to see if anyone was watching. The neighborhood Christmas lights were off, the houselights were off, even the few porch lights that stayed on late were off. Only the streetlight broke the darkness, casting pools of pale light through the thin fog.

He was safe. No one could see him. He shook himself off, tucked himself back inside his flannel pajamas, reached to close the window— and froze.

There was movement on the roof of the house across the street.

Well, not a house, actually. It was too big to be a house. It was the Sutter place, which his mother used to call, "the only bona fide mansion on the Central Oregon Coast." Later when he learned the history of it, when he was older and into such things, he discovered that his mother had been wrong –there had been other mansions, just none as visible, none quite as centrally located as the one on the street below their little two-bedroom ranch.

Still he struggled, trying to get the window closed, the wind blowing against him, plastering the ice-cold snap buttons against his bare chest. Somehow the battle became him against the window, and he was losing.

Then he saw the movement again. And what had looked like shadows became three men dressed as Santa Claus, dark sacks against their backs, struggling with the dormer on the side of the house.

He watched, horrified, as they tugged it open. Then they disappeared inside, one by one, none of them looking up at him, none of them noticing.

Then, from inside, white-gloved hands pulled the dormer closed.

***

OH, TOMMY DID ALL THE RIGHT THINGS. He woke his parents, who called the police. His dad stared out the bathroom window a long time, as if he could see something different. Tommy stared too, pointed out the sleigh on the front lawn, saying it hadn't been there when he saw the men, but his dad just ignored him.

So did the police after they arrived. They walked around the Sutter place, saw no evidence of false entry, saw nothing out of the ordinary, and said so. They came up to Tommy's house, listened to his story, and told his parents not to let him watch so much television.

Then they left.

Tommy's mom made him use the bathroom one more time before he went to bed. No one had closed the window and as he looked out on the mansion below, he saw that the sleigh was gone.

Only this time, he didn't tell anyone. He snuck back to bed, pulled the covers to his chin, and shivered for the rest of the night.

***

CHRISTMAS WAS NEVER THE SAME after that. Tommy made sure there were no Santa Claus decorations in the house. He wouldn't sit on the Santa man's lap at the mall, and he wouldn't watch any Santa shows on television. He told his parents that he didn't believe, and they seemed saddened by it, but they thought it understandable.

After all, the Sutter place had been robbed that night. Apparently the police had arrived too late to do anything about it. Tommy had seen something. Turned out the dormer window was askew. There was even a bit of extra ash in the fireplace that next morning, and men's shoe prints tracking all over the house.

One of the police officers came by to apologize and to take Tommy's statement again. The theory was that the men had used the Santa Claus outfits as a ruse to get into the house, figuring they could pose on the roof like Christmas decorations if a car went by.

Brilliant, the police called it.

Humbug, Tommy would have said to himself if he had known the word then. Complete and total humbug.

He had seen the dark side of Santa, and was never ever going to be the same again.

***

CHILDHOOD LOST, CYNICISM FOUND. Outwardly Tommy Ulrick was the same as all the other little boys of his age, unless someone mentioned Santa Claus. It got so bad that his parents used to warn people not to use the name. At Christmas, he became sullen and fearful, and there didn't seem to be anything anyone could do about it.

His parents thought he would grow out of it. It was a phase, they said, brought on by a traumatic childhood event, and, as Tommy got older and realized that his attitude toward the Jolly Old Elf was socially unacceptable, he stopped talking about it.

Instead, he turned inward. He studied. He learned everything he could about the enemy, and what he saw he didn't like.

It was, he came to understand, the biggest fraud ever perpetrated on the public. A round-cheeked old man masquerading as a saint who gave toys to children, all the while using those children to hide his own greed. In fact, the old man used his scam to teach greed.

In Tommy—now Thomas—Ulrick's life, Christmas ceased to be about love and peace and goodwill toward all men. Instead, it turned into a holiday about stuff. Who bought the most, who spent the most, who got the most. Even people who belonged to other religions gave into the Christmas frenzy. They treated it as a secular holiday, so their kids wouldn't be left out of the stuff-getting.

It was, Thomas realized, a shameful thing.

And when he turned thirty, he'd finally had enough.

***

LATER, HE FIGURED, everything culminated that year. His parents had died in a car accident the year before. He'd taken a leave of absence from his big city reporter's position—a forced leave of absence: reporters are supposed to do everything they can to get a story, but apparently "everything" did *not* include breaking a few minor privacy laws. His third fiancée left him just like all the others had when she realized that he hated Christmas. Apparently his fiancées could tolerate different religions, different attitudes toward money, but not a bah-humbugish attitude toward Christmas.

It was, he discovered, the ultimate deal-breaker.

So on Christmas Eve of that year, he sat down at his kitchen table, in his comfortable two-bedroom ranch style house in the Portland suburb of Beaverton, and, like he used to do when he was starting an article, made a list.

1. Adults all acknowledge there is no Santa Claus.
2. Children are encouraged to believe in Santa Claus.
3. Santa doesn't give gifts. Parents do, thus perpetuating the myth.
4. From Halloween on, people see Santa Claus on the streets, and think nothing of it.
5. People decorate their homes with Santa Claus iconography, making it easy for fake Santas to hide.
6. The only thing that people do when they see a Santa is give him something. (Does the Salvation Army really still exist? Do they sanction those little red change boxes? Is this a direct part of the scam or is this something else encouraged by the Evil Santa Brigade?)
7. Was the lump of coal more than a metaphor? Perhaps, in the early years, the Santa thieves left only a lump of coal when they cleaned out a house.

8. Naughty or nice. Who's to determine? Based on what criteria?

9. Robberies increase supposedly because houses are more vulnerable. People in the holiday spirit aren't as vigilant.

10. Fires increase. Arson to cover up robberies?

11. More people commit suicide during the holidays than at any other time of the year. Real suicides? Or more cover-ups—killed when they discover someone who isn't supposed to be in the house?

12. Was Clement Moore in on this?

13. How long has this been going on?

Thomas stopped, chilled to the bone. One man against a centuries-old tradition of duplicity and thievery.

He had to stop this. But how?

***

It came to him as he woke up the next morning. There had to be a grain of truth to everything in the myth.

He sat up, his frayed cotton sheets pooled around his waist. He was willing to believe that the original Santa thieves went down chimneys, just like the stories. A roof was a great access point for a robber, and a hundred years ago, children used to climb into chimneys to clean them. Skinny children, but children nonetheless. He didn't believe that fat old men slid down chimneys—but that was the impossibility that made the idea seem so ludicrous. Better to go back to the truth.

And he would wager that a lot of Santa's Helpers went through the front doors too.

He rubbed his hands together. He felt like he was finally onto something.

He got out of bed, and grabbed his robe, sliding it on as he made his way to the kitchen. He didn't believe that Santa operated from the North Pole—too cold, too remote, too impractical—but he would wager that there was a hideout. It didn't have to be very big—not like the factory portrayed in all those stupid Christmas movies. After all, Santa wasn't making toys. He was stealing stuff.

The hideout had to be a place to run to, a place to hide, a place to split up the wealth, like the Hole-in-the-Wall of Western Outlaw lore.

And if he found the Hole in the Wall, the hideout, he found the bad guys.

He had the power to stop this scam once and for all.

***

IT WAS EASIER THAN HE THOUGHT. It just took time.

After all, he had data from thirty years of collecting. His newspaper training made him an excellent sleuth. He searched for robberies, fires, and suicides, throwing in a few surprise deaths from heart failure and a couple of thwarted attempts.

He made a cybermap and marked out all the hits in the United States for the last fifty years, searching for a pattern—and what he found terrified him. If his assumptions were true, and he had no reason to think they weren't—then he was dealing with something so large that he could barely contemplate it.

Every state got hit, every county, every town—and in the right statistical proportions. In fact, that's what gave the plot away. The statistics were too perfect. No cluster of suicides in Denver in any one year, for example, or no extra fires in San Jose. Apparently the statisticians hadn't noticed that every city had just about the same number of robberies, deaths, and fires in the weeks before Christmas. The ever-so-slight variations came from what he would consider to be unconnected events— gang killings, insurance fraud arson, and the robberies caused by non-affiliated thieves (whom, he noted, usually got caught).

He expanded his search to include Britain and Western Europe, and found fewer incidences there, although those too were statistically perfect. Going back a hundred years, he found higher incidences in England; he figured that was probably where the scam originated.

Thomas spent weeks analyzing the information and figured that the hideout was in the United States where the pickings were good. There were probably several sub-hideouts, but the main one—if he were the guy planning all of this—had to be centrally located.

Unless…

He paused, hands over the keys, as inspiration struck again.

All those greeting cards, posters, t-shirts. *Images* everywhere of Santa in a swimsuit and loud floral-print shirt, lounging in a beach chair on the sand, chubby ankles crossed while he stared at a pristine ocean. Those pictures never depicted Santa on a Hawaiian beach or relaxing on California's sultry sands.

Santa was always in Florida, generally Miami Beach, and he was always grinning at the camera.

Taunting someone—taunting Thomas—to find him.

Thomas scanned the Florida information. The farther south he went, the more evidence he found—in the lack of evidence, of course. Fewer Christmas fires (statistically attributable to the warm weather, the lack of heaters, the fact that Christmas trees didn't dry out as quickly), fewer suicides (statistically attributable the advanced age of the population; if they lived that long, they wouldn't throw what was left away), and surprisingly, given the wealth of the area, fewer robberies (statistically attributable to the fact that most people traveled *to* Florida during the holidays; fewer vacant homes). Heart attacks were up, but they didn't fall into his mathematical model because very few of those were a surprise, again given the advance age of the population.

He went to his hardcopy cabinet and pulled one of his many Santa souvenirs out of the postcard file. Santa, wearing sunglasses five times too big, a red-and-orange checked shirt a size too small, and matching orange shorts which revealed pale hairy legs, waved out of the image. *Wish You Were Here,* said the red lettering across the top.

"I will be," he promised the Jolly Old Elf. "Soon."

∗∗∗

FOR SOME REASON, the thievery began again in Gainesville. Orlando was safe—maybe because Santa liked it there, or spread out his Florida vacation spots–but anything north of Gainesville was as fair as the rest of the western world.

He spent the months before Christmas studying the maps, searching for patterns. He finally found them. Simple, elegant, and difficult to see. The thieves worked in an alphabetical or numerical pattern by street name. Each state was assigned a letter or number, and then the pattern shifted clockwise from year to year. In other words, if Main was the "A" street in the first year, the next year it would be the "Z" street. The pattern worked the same with numbers.

Once the state's number or letter had been assigned, the thieves picked the exact street according to housing prices and the quality of the neighborhood. Then they probably staked a few houses out. It sounded like a lot of work, but it wasn't.

If he was right, that year Florida was the "D" street and the "30th" state. Gainesville was a number town— there were a lot of thirties. Southwest thirties, thirties with streets, thirties with avenues. Thomas scanned all the possible thirties and came up with what he considered to be a jackpot—30th Terrace, an area where the homes were worth half a million or more with lots of acreage, right in the middle of the city. Right smack in the center of that region was a house that had been owned for a couple of decades by the same people, philanthropists by their profile, who didn't believe in home security systems.

He did a bit more research, discovered that the home's owners boarded their dog and canceled their newspaper delivery every year just before Christmas. He didn't even break a sweat to find out that information. He imagined the Santa Stealers had all of this down to a science.

On December 18, he had lunch with fiancée number three—for old times sake, he said—and told her he was going out of town. He gave her a key to his safe deposit box, and told her to open it if he wasn't back by the first of the year.

She looked at him as if he were crazy, which was how she had been looking at him for the last year or more. But she agreed, which was all that mattered.

Then he flew to Orlando, rented a black sports car, and drove to Gainesville.

***

HE HADN'T DONE A REAL honest-to-god stakeout in nearly five years. Back when he was young and hungry, he got a lot of his information just spying on people. The older he got, the more he used legal information obtained through records, and then as he learned his way around computers, he found more and more fascinating things illegally.

But this was no longer a computer sort of case. This required diligence, wakefulness, and quick-thinking.

He slept during the day at a cheap hotel on the highway and watched the empty house at night. No neighbors nearby to report him, no big dogs to bark. By December 22nd, he was beginning to think the house was too perfect, or his research suspect. He hadn't seen hide nor hair of a sleigh or eight tiny reindeer or anything else near the target house.

But he knew that these Santa Bandits struck all the way through December 25th. He just had to be patient.

And finally, at 4 a.m. on the morning of December 24th, his patience paid off. He was keeping himself awake by making condensation rings on the driver's side window, when he heard a car engine, a sound he hadn't heard after midnight in this neighborhood since he started his vigil.

He slumped down in the sports car's bucket seat, and watched as a dark colored late model minivan with its lights off pulled into the house's long gravel driveway. When he was sure the occupants could no longer see his car, he grabbed his binoculars and climbed over the shifting column to the passenger seat. There he leaned against the dash and watched.

A chill ran up his spine, and for a moment, he touched his six-year-old self.

Instead he focused on the movement he saw on the empty house's roof. Three men, just like he had seen twenty-four years before, dressed as Santa, carrying black bags over their shoulders—empty bags. The men balanced precariously on the steep roof, climbing to its peak. Then the first man reached over and pulled open a window that probably led to an attic. He slid in, head first, as if he were diving into a pool.

The other two followed.

And Thomas, his six-year-old self still closer to the surface than he wanted the boy to be, slipped out of the car to pee.

***

LESS THAN AN HOUR LATER, the men emerged the way they entered, full bags over their shoulders. They slid down the back roof, presumably to the van, which he hadn't been able to see.

Then, lights out, it left the driveway.

Thomas waited until it was nearly a block away before he started the rental. He followed, his lights out too, keeping a discreet distance.

The van's lights came on at the end of 30th Terrace, and from then on all driving was normal. Thomas tailed them, mentally congratulating himself for a) practicing that skill a lot before and b) renting a sports car. He was able to keep up.

As he drove, he called 911 and reported the break-in. Step one of his plan.

Just as he expected, when they hit the highway, they headed south. But they didn't go to Miami, like he expected.

Instead, they went to Orlando, where the waiters sang, men dressed like giant mice, and make-believe was part of the air.

His enemy was craftier than even Thomas thought. He should have known that Miami Beach was a ruse. It was the Florida part with the grain of truth to it.

When they finally stopped, he felt a surge of disappointment. He couldn't help himself. He had been hoping for something interesting, something unique.

Instead, they pulled into a strip mall in one of the outlying areas of Orlando, where the rents were cheaper and the businesses cheesier. They drove around back and he followed, but he knew where they were going. He didn't have to be a rocket scientist to figure that one out.

The biggest store on the strip. It had a candy-cane striped door, giant toy soldiers guarding either side. Decorated Christmas trees stood in front of each window, and a couple of plaster elves looked like they had just finished painting the store's name on its sign: *The Christmas Cottage*.

But that wasn't the biggest giveaway. The biggest giveaway were the Santa statues—all three of them. On the roof.

***

THOMAS HAD HIS VIDEO CAMERA, his microcassette tape recorder, and a digital camera with a telephoto lens. As he got out of the car, he called 911, said he saw some suspicious activity at the Christmas Cottage, and that he was getting out of his car to investigate.

The dispatch urged him not to, of course, but he hung up, as if he were a zealous citizen. Which, he supposed, he was.

He left the digital zoom in the car, clicked on the microcassette recorder, and headed toward the back. The sun was just starting to come up, sending pale yellow light across the flat Florida landscape.

As he expected, the van was parked directly behind the Christmas Cottage. The store's back doors were open, and no one was in sight.

He slipped inside. The back of the store was bigger than he thought, almost a store in and of itself. There was an assortment of boxes, all of them clearly merchandise, some open with ornaments or tinsel hanging out. But an open storage door on the left side revealed items that didn't belong in a Christmas store.

He moved toward it as quietly as he could. Voices were coming from the storefront, talking amiably, as if someone were telling a story. Probably relating the events of the night.

When he got closer to the storage door, he stopped and made sure he was in shadow. He needed a place to hide if the thieves came back. He found the perfect spot behind a man-sized box, and set to work.

With shaking hands he raised the video camera to his right eye. Mentally, he cataloged as he went: coin collections, artwork, and jewelry—so much jewelry that his entire body felt numb. Then there were silver—from flatware to pitchers, the antiques (all small enough to carry), and the occasional high-end television.

He was nearly done with a white-gloved hand grabbed his wrist, pulling the camcorder down.

"Ho, ho, ho," a deep voice said with more cheer than seemed appropriate to the situation.

Another hand took the camcorder away. Thomas started to protest, but stopped. He was busted. He had to think clearly now.

He turned slowly, and tried not to let his surprise show.

The man standing behind him was no more than five feet tall, with white hair down to his shoulders and a fluffy white beard. He was wearing a red suit with real fur, and shiny black boots. He ho-hoed again and his stomach jiggled, just like that infamous bowl full of jelly. He had an unlit pipe in his bow-shaped mouth, and his blue eyes did twinkle merrily—at Thomas's expense.

All of the images of Santa were on the mark—if one ignored the height problem.

"Little Tommy Ulrick," the man said. "I wondered if you would be a problem."

"H-How do you know who I am?" Thomas asked.

The man tsk-tsked. "Tommy, of all people, you have to ask? I'm Santa. I know everything."

"Yeah," Thomas said, blessing his own forethought in having the microcassette recorder running. "That's why you have to steal for a living."

Claus—or whoever he was—sighed. "Ah, an explanation man. Somehow I would have thought you had it all worked out, Tommy."

"Thomas. And all I want to know is why."

"Not how? Not all the particulars?"

"No," Thomas said. He finally had control of his voice again. "Only why."

Claus's twinkling eyes narrowed. "I wouldn't have figured you for a true believer."

"I'm not," Thomas said. "I'm a reporter. I have a Need to Know."

Claus made a rude sound. "A need to spy, you mean. Which I would have thought that incident when you were six cured you of."

"Naw," Thomas said. "Just made me even more curious. So. Why do you do it?"

Claus sighed. "I hate this part."

His friends came through the doorway. They were even shorter. Even though they were wearing jeans and ratty Marlins t-shirts, they looked like Santa's elves. Which they probably were.

"Another one, Boss?"

"Whatcha gonna do this time?"

Claus ignored them. Instead he stared at Thomas. "Look, I'll split the loot with you fifty-fifty if you just don't ask for the explanation."

"Too late," Thomas said. "I already did."

One of the elves laughed. "Gotta tell him, Boss. Don't you just hate those magic rules?"

"How much time do we have?" the other elf asked.

"If he called 911, maybe ten more minutes."

"Plenty of time, Boss."

"Someone trained you, right?" Thomas asked. "This is like a worldwide scam that's been going on for centuries. The original Santa was, what? a real Fagan? A man who trained his cohorts from childhood?"

"I am the original Santa," Claus said.

This time it was Thomas's turn to make the rude noise.

"I *am*," Claus said. He turned to the elves. "I really do hate this part."

"Get it over with, Boss," the first elf said, then crossed his arms and leaned against the wall. "I'm keeping an ear out for the coppers."

"Pigs," the other elf corrected.

Thomas frowned at them. Coppers? Pigs? Was their slang really out of date? Or were they faking it just for him?

"You figured it out," Claus said. "You know that part of the myth is true, and part of it is convenient. Well, I'm just a jolly old elf. Really."

"More like a leprechaun," the elf said.

"Or even that Coyote character," the other elf said.

"A trickster?" Thomas asked. That part he hadn't figured out.

Claus put one finger beside his nose and pointed at Thomas with the other hand. Thomas ducked, as if he expected something magical to happen to him.

Claus chuckled, a deep rolling laugh that seemed to fill the room. "You *do* believe."

"I knew something was up," Thomas said. "I figured out your theft pattern. I know about your units. I even figured you were in Florida."

"But you don't know why, and it bothers you." Claus let his fingers drop.

"Yes," Thomas said, if he could keep the trio talking, they'd stay here until the cops arrived. Then he'd have everything on tape. "If you have magic, why steal?"

"Magic requires belief. A few people still believe, but for the most part, rationalists have taken over. About the time Claus started, don't you know."

Thomas did know. He just hadn't put it together.

"So," Claus said, "if I can get people to believe in a jolly old elf for part of a year, why then, I have a bit of my powers. Not all, any more. Just enough."

"But why use them to steal?"

Claus frowned. "An immortal has-been needs a way to maintain his lifestyle."

"At the expense of people's homes? At the expense of their lives?"

"Oh, crap, Boss," one of the elves said. "This is a live one."

Claus continued to ignore them. "Mistakes happen," he said. "The deaths are always regrettable."

"Regrettable?" Thomas's voice rose. Then he cleared his throat, too late, of course. They'd probably already heard the panic.

"I think I hear sirens, Boss," one of the elves said.

"Me too." The second elf's ears—which really were pointed—started to twitch.

"You go," Claus said. "I'll handle this guy."

"Boss, we're going to need a new hideout," the first elf said.

"We'll worry about that later. Just go."

They scurried out the back and closed the double doors. After a moment, Thomas heard the van start.

Claus was smiling at him. It wasn't a nice smile. "I have so many options. I could let those cops you called find you here with the loot. I could kill you. Or I could make use of you."

"You'd make me a part of your thieving band?"

"Don't be silly," Claus said. "You wouldn't last a year. I can see through to Naughty and Nice, and you got waaaay too much Nice in you. That's probably why you searched me out, even though you say it's for the story."

He squeezed Thomas's wrist just a little harder. For an old man, he was very strong.

"Story," Claus muttered. "I wish I could use you for the story. But times have changed."

"Is that what the elves were alluding to? Someone else has caught you?"

"You'll kick yourself when I tell you." Claus grinned. His teeth were pointed, almost fanged. Thomas wondered how he ever found this face pleasant.

"Clement Moore," Thomas said softly.

"Twas the Night Before Christmas. Same day, different year. Different century." Claus tilted his head, looking thoughtful. "Didn't have computers then. We weren't as accurate in knowing who'd be home and who wouldn't be. *He* had children I could threaten. You keep losing your fiancées."

"You know that?"

"My mind is full of useless information, all of it relating to goodness or badness. You'd think magic would be great—and it probably would if someone got the stuff of stories, you know, the ability to make things disappear, being able to fly things across a room. But no. I get stupid talents. Seeing people while they sleep. They lay in one position for a while, sigh, and roll over. Nothing exciting there. And the naughty and nice stuff? Good for the occasional blackmail, but nothing more."

Claus rolled his tiny eyes. Thomas strained to hear those sirens. But he couldn't, not yet. How good were those elven ears?

"I'd like to pat you on the head and tell you to write a nice poem, filled with *my* lies, of course, and a little bit of the truth," Claus said. "But these days, the myth-making machine is self-generating. Who'd've known what a boon television would be?"

"Who'd've known?" Thomas asked. He swallowed, wondering if he could shake himself free, and get out those double doors before the Jolly Old Elf caught him. Probably. It would be worth a try.

"So," Claus said, "I think I'll just let you go."

Thomas had been concentrating so much on escaping that he almost missed what Claus said. "What?"

"I'm letting you go." Claus dropped Thomas's wrist like it contaminated him. "Toddle on."

"But they'll catch you."

"No, they won't," Claus said, going to the storage area, dropping and locking the door.

"I'll tell," Thomas said.

"Of course you will." Claus grinned. "But who's going to believe you?"

***

No ONE, IT TURNED OUT. Not the cops who showed up, only to be greeted by the big man himself ("Sorry to bother you, officers. We got an early morning shipment and this man was worried."), not Thomas's old editor ("Tom, I say this only as a friend. Counseling. Lots of counseling.") and especially not fiancée number three ("Don't ever call me again. Ever!").

In the end, there was nothing he could do. Oh, he called and reported a few break-ins before they occurred, but that only got him brought him to the attention of the police –and not in a good way. And then he tried to warn potential victims, which only made his police surveillance worse. He soon figured that if he continued along this path, he would soon be arrested for the crimes himself.

And to make matters worse, every January, he got a postcard from Florida—that year's Santa postcard, which always had the happy *Wish You Were Here!* on the front. On the back was just a scrawled number.

That first year he had no idea what the number meant. But the second year, after he mapped the robberies, he knew.

Total profits, after expenses, of course. Never less than ten million dollars. Tax free.

The old guy could have quit years ago. But he didn't. He wasn't doing it for the money. He was addicted to the belief.

And Thomas, whom everyone doubted, understood why.

Rehabilitation

THIS CHRISTMAS WAS DIFFERENT. For the first time in fifteen years, he had a choice of jobs. *Help Wanted* signs littered Portland. From restaurants to boutiques, from offices to museums, the red signs with the outlined white lettering beckoned from every window.

But Matt took the job he had taken every year since he started wandering. It still shocked him how quickly the malls hired their Santas, how little time these places, which entrusted other people's children to big men with appealing laughs, spent on researching their employees' backgrounds. When he had started in 1984, barely twenty and hardly large enough to play Santa, computers were rare things, personal data hard to trace. But it wasn't now, and lawsuits were more common. Sometimes he wondered how many of his colleagues in their red suits with fake white fur trim had records, and how many of them used the information they got from a tyke in ways that would have made the real Santa leave coal in their stockings.

He liked playing Santa; it was the only time he felt as if he had worth. Every year, he heard from the mall manager that he was the best Santa the mall had ever had, and every year he promised to return the next, and every year, he was somewhere else, with a different name, and a different story. It used to be that he would arrive in his new home with a different dream, but at thirty-five, he was getting too old for dreams. Dreams were a luxury a man like him should never indulge in.

His résumé said nothing about his real past, of course. This year's named him Matthew J. Sturtz, a man who had graduated from the University of Oregon with a Ph.D. in English, who had spent most of his years as a professor of English Literature at Gustavus Adolphus. He was taking a sabbatical, his résumé said, returning to his home state to write the definitive paper on Herman Melville's "Bartleby the Scrivener," and even though he had only been here a month, he already felt the need for a diversion, a way to interact with people, to get out now and then.

He had learned, over the years, that such unusual detail—along with the correct addresses and phone numbers—got him a long way in the Santa business. Most false names were common ones, easy to spell, so he always chose something like Sturtz. Most fake résumés were filled with jobs impossible to check, so he made his easy to check, out of state, and plausible, so plausible in fact that most personnel managers never bothered. When quizzed, he had his answers down so pat, that nothing surprised him. He spent October studying

Melville and "Bartleby"—he could discuss both with pedantic enthusiasm, guaranteed to make the interviewer's eyes glaze within thirty seconds.

If Matt did his job right—and he always did—the interviewer had no suspicions about him at all. If Matt did his job right, the interviewer would always end the interview with, "You're exactly the kind of man we want playing Santa. Please go downstairs. They'll brief you on everything you'll need."

The mall that hired him as one of this year's rotating Santas was one of the oldest in Portland. It had five anchor stores, two stories, and a new wing. An atrium, with a high-domed glass ceiling, in the center of the mall provided the space for his little kingdom: a throne-sized chair with two large cushions, a giant Christmas tree—real, he soon learned, with that wonderful fresh scent—and a pile of presents stacked beneath it, each marked with a child's sex and age, each donated by a different store.

This place had spent a lot of money on the costumes too: no fake white fluff that had pilled or grown gray with time. White fur instead—not real, of course, but the kind that covered the best stuffed animals. The suits were red velvet, the beards and wigs from a men's costume shop that guaranteed authenticity. When Matt applied the spirit gum, he felt as if he were going to go on stage instead of into the sunlit atrium with a gaggle of kids waiting to sit on his lap.

His first day, the day after Thanksgiving, went well, as did his second, and third. No baby peed on him, no frightened toddler kicked him in the wrong place, no angry parent returned demanding a different present for his precious little darling. Each night, Matt returned to home—one of the hotels near the airport that catered to out-of-towners who rented by the week—put his feet up on the presswood coffee table, feeling as if he'd had real human contact, as if things—for this one brief instant— were good once again.

He knew it was an illusion, and that come December 25th, the illusion would evaporate as if it had never been. Matt Sturtz would become someone else, would live somewhere else, and gradually lose the comfort the season had given him.

He knew all that, and he no longer minded. It was the rhythm of his life, the only tradition he had, and he valued it, above all else.

***

ON TUESDAY, DECEMBER FIRST, the rain came down in sheets, and the bus driver, obviously new, struggled to keep the Metro on the slick roads. Drivers honked and cursed, pedestrians stood away from the curbs to keep from getting splashed, and Matt had to walk the last three blocks to make sure he was on time to work.

In the locker room, the previous Santa was hanging up his uniform. He was an older man, a grandfather or so he said, who loved spending time with children. He grinned when he saw Matt close the filthy metal door and grab the handle of the dented locker the mall had provided him and his precious suit.

"Not a lot of business," the grandfather said, "but I'll bet it'll pick up tonight."

"It usually does," Matt said, and then turned his back as he pulled off his jeans. Some of the Santas wore their jeans under the suit, but the kids could always see that. By the time he had finished changing, the grandfather was gone.

Matt applied his beard, mustache and wig, always amazed that with the right facial hair, he could look forty years older than he really was. He practiced the eye twinkle in the scratched mirror above the sink, then put on his cap, and let himself out of the locker room.

Here, in the mall proper, he was Santa. He walked with a joy he never had anywhere else. He smiled at children, and ho-ho-ho-ed on command. As he made his way past the decorated fake trees in the center of the mall, past the women with strollers, the men looking harried, he assisted in little ways. He helped catch a two-year-old who was on a shrieking, giggling tear away from her father who was trying to adjust the infant he carried in a neck sling. As the man tried to express his gratitude, Matt moved on. He caught a package that an overloaded business woman dropped, and then he was at his location.

The piped-in music in this part of the mall had class; Frank Sinatra singing "Have Yourself a Merry Little Christmas" which, Matt knew, would be followed by Ella

Fitzgerald wondering "What Are You Doing New Year's Eve?" He appreciated that. There were only so many Muzak renditions of "Jingle Bells" that a man could experience in one lifetime.

The throne was comfortable, and the elf, a middle-aged librarian with a knack for keeping people in line, grinned at him as he settled in. There was no line at the moment: there probably wouldn't be until parents got off work—most of the stay-at-home parents were preparing dinner—and it was too early for the last-minute shoppers to crowd the mall. He had an hour or more to keep himself occupied before the first real busy session started.

From the throne, he could see the nearby stores: the Lord & Taylor anchor store with its male and female dummies wearing Christmas evening wear, gold garlands around the windows, and expensive gifts under a very real, very large tree; the Musicland beside it, the window garish with red and green and white peppermint paper; the Waldenbooks on the other side, its display filled with coffee-table books that people would look at once and then never touch again.

He imagined having a gift list, shopping, as so many men did now, hurrying from his 9 to 5 for an hour at the mall before stopping for take-out Chinese on the way home. He wondered if he would have been that kind of husband, that sort of father, the one who was involved, who wore a baby in a sling around his neck while chasing a joyful toddler. He wondered and felt the familiar twist in his heart, and then made himself think of something else.

If he turned ever so slightly in the throne, he could see the stores with the outdoor access: the photographer on the corner, advertising family portraits; the jeweler who specialized in diamonds and easy credit; the beauty shop that also did nails. They were empty as well.

He suppressed a sigh and the elf grinned at him. It was an infectious grin with its own twinkle, and it made him wonder if she felt discriminated against, if she thought she could be as good—or better—a Santa than he could.

He smiled back, then glanced at the double doors at the other side of the anchor store. Cars were cruising the rain-soaked parking lot. A van with bald tires screeched so loudly as it stopped that it nearly drowned out Ella. The man who got out of the passenger's side was little more than a boy, really, a teenager who had gotten his height, but hadn't gotten rid of the lanky gawkiness that marked him as a stranger in his newer bigger body. He pulled his battered leather jacket around him as he ran into the jewelry store, pausing to look at the engagement rings in the display beside the window, before going in where Matt could no longer see him.

Getting engaged at Christmas. All the hopes and dreams and special moments tied together. The twist again, so fierce that he had to turn away. He faced the main section of the mall, saw the father he had rescued, the baby now asleep against his chest, the little girl pointing at the tree. The father grinned at Matt, Matt grinned back, and suddenly, he was in business.

***

It was as if the magic held him in those hours, the heart-warming magic found only in hour-long T.V. shows and the annual holiday Disney movies. He could believe that each child who sat on his lap would go home to a large tree, with ample presents beneath, loving parents, a new year destined to be filled with only joy. The grubby hands pulling on his beard, the candy-soured breath, whispering important secrets that usually showed the triumph of marketing in the American psyche, somehow gave him reassurance that in other homes, at least, something wonderful was happening, something he could share for a brief moment, and that, he assured himself, was enough.

Matt always insisted on telling his elf the child's wishes so that the elf could tell the parents when she handed out the present; that way he had done his duty as only Santa could. The hours went quickly, the eager faces blurred, and when the line finally dwindled to nothing, he felt a healthy exhaustion that he never got when he worked construction or got the odd bartending job.

He leaned back in his throne, glanced at his watch, and saw he had fifteen minutes until the mall closed.

"You didn't even take a break," his elf said. "I suppose you could now. I doubt we'll get anyone else."

In his mind's eye, he saw an imaginary tow-headed boy, dragging his tired mother through the large mall, only to arrive at Santa's Village to find Santa's throne empty.

He smiled. "I can last fifteen more minutes."

"I'm not sure I can," she said and wiped her forehead with the back of her hand. She had to move more than he did.

"Go," he said. "I doubt I'll get a rush."

She shook her head. "We're a team," she said, and sat on the tiny red and green chair to the side of him, looking as if she would wilt before the shift was up.

He couldn't watch her or his own tiredness would overwhelm him. Instead he watched the stores closing: the Lord & Taylor's employees waiting impatiently by their cash registers; the Waldenbooks manager dragging her display shelf inside the store; the last stragglers in Musicland. The photographer had closed an hour before, and the beautician just after dinner. Only the jewelry store had its display lights on and the door to the street open.

The van was parked outside, near a streetlight, its single unbroken taillight turning the rain red. Exhaust fumes floated like fog over the pavement, and Matt frowned as he watched. The boy apparently hadn't bought his ring yet, or was coming back for another look.

A different teenage boy appeared from the driver's side. He grabbed the silver handle on the van's back and pulled the door open. The interior light didn't come on, but the streetlight provided just enough illumination to reveal several shotguns, handguns, and some ammunition.

"What are you looking at?" Matt's elf asked.

"Get mall security," he said, rising as he did so, "and dial 911."

Maybe he was making things up. Maybe. But his instincts told him that this was too odd to be coincidental. And his instincts had been on more than off these past fifteen years. Besides, he knew something about teenagers, shotguns, and determination. He put the red velvet rope with the *Santa Will Be Right Back* sign across the edge of the line, and walked to the jewelry store.

He didn't want to seem like he was coming to the rescue. That could make things messy. Instead, he played a new role: Santa as Christmas shopper. As he walked past the giant tree, he carefully bent over and whispered to the woman who was sitting on the fake park bench to get out of the way, something bad was going to happen, and to, as inconspicuously as she could, make sure no one else was in this vicinity.

She frowned at him as if he were crazy, then she looked over his shoulder. She must have seen the boys in the haze of the streetlight for she nodded once, stood, and walked toward a couple nuzzling near the packages.

The employee in the jewelry store, a slender woman whose hair was slipping out of its careful bun, was matching receipts to the cash register tape, an old-fashioned procedure not really necessary in these days of computers. Only a jewelry store would still continue that old-fashioned practice; it had high mark-up and low volume.

Outside, one of the boys slid his shotgun inside his open jacket. Matt made himself look away. He entered the jewelry store, whistling "Frosty the Snowman" and the clerk looked up, clearly startled. She opened her mouth, probably to tell him they were closing, when Matt smiled.

"Hello there!" Matt said in his jolliest voice. "I came to look at your engagement rings."

Without waiting for her response, he walked past the counter. "Get down," he whispered. "And look natural as you do it."

He didn't watch to see if she followed his instruction. Instead, he walked to the engagement ring display with its garish *Pay Nothing Until July!* sign.

The other boy closed the back of the van and joined his partner. They headed toward the store.

Matt reached up and hit the button that activated the mesh gate. It started down, too slowly for his comfort. The boys looked startled, then one of them grinned, pulled open the outside door, and slid under the gate.

The other boy followed.

On the mall side of the store, a second gate fell. Matt hadn't planned on that.

"Trying to be a hero, Pops?" the first boy asked as he pulled the shotgun out of his coat.

The clerk gasped, and Matt yelled, "Get down!" in case she hadn't hidden already. The gates made it all the way to the floor, clanging, trapping them inside.

The first boy held the shotgun on Matt. "You don't do nothing, Pops and everything'll be fine." He inclined his head toward his friend. "You," he said, smart enough not to use names, even though he didn't seem to care about hiding his acne scarred face. "Get the stuff."

The second boy had a sack, a red velvet one that look too similar to a Santa sack for comfort. He opened the display of diamond bracelets on the other side of the door, and began yanking them out.

Perhaps it was the bag. Perhaps it was the realization that these were boys, and inexperienced ones at that. Perhaps it was the knowledge that the clerk was safe, and whatever happened to Matt didn't matter. No one would care. No one would mourn. He was free to do as he wished, and what he wished was to stop this now.

Adrenaline pumped through him. He moved quicker than he thought he ever could.

He grabbed the engagement ring display case, and tossed it at the boy with the shotgun. The boy whirled, wasn't quick enough to shoot or get out of the way. The display hit him in the stomach and the gun fell out of his fingers, sliding on the red indoor-outdoor carpet.

Matt dove for the gun, and came up holding it, feeling absurdly like Rambo in a Santa costume. Time had slowed to a crawl—only once before had time done that to him—and it felt like each breath, each movement took a year.

The clerk screamed, and Matt shouted at the second boy to "Hold it!" The boy looked up and, startled, dropped the sack. He reached for the handgun he had stuck in his waistband.

"Touch it," Matt said, "and I will shoot you."

The boy held out his hands and slowly raised them, western-style. The other boy on the floor was struggling to get the display case off him, moaning as he did so, diamond rings scattered about him like shards of glass.

The sirens started first, coming closer and closer. Red and blue lights played across the cars outside, and Matt turned just enough to see mall security, watching through the mesh. The clerk, who still clutched her receipts, had her mouth open, her lower jaw trembling as if she had palsy.

"Let them in," Matt said.

It took a moment for his command to register, but when it did, she used a different control to open the gate on the mall side. The security cop came in, carrying the handcuffs he'd probably never used. He looked at Matt for instruction, and Matt nodded at the standing boy first.

"He's got a gun," Matt said, and the guard slipped a tentative hand around the boy's waist, grabbed the gun with two fingers, and, without taking his gaze off the boy's face, stepped backwards to set the gun on the counter.

For a moment Matt thought the boy would make a lunge for it, but he glanced at Matt and apparently didn't like what he saw there, so he didn't move. The first boy didn't seem to notice. The display had injured him somehow. He had stopped trying to move it, and had lain down in the position he had been in, still moaning quietly.

The red-and-blue lights filled the interior of the store, winking garishly off the diamonds, making Matt feel suddenly as if he were in a badly designed disco. The guard grabbed the boy and cuffed him, then the real cops came in the mall side, and took over, now that it was too late.

***

Two hours of story-telling in the manager's office, sitting in the only comfortable chair, looking at the out-of-date notices on the bulletin board flapping in the breeze coming out of a poorly placed heating duct. The cops who took his statement were sympathetic: they were the ones who had come on the scene, and they praised him for his quick thinking, his decision to trap the robbers, his whispered instructions to the elf, the customers, the clerk. But they said, because they had to, because it was true, sometimes things don't end so well. Sometimes the boy with the gun knows how to shoot, sometimes a well-pushed display case isn't very heavy at all, sometimes the other boy pays attention. You could have died, she could have died, and for what? Some franchise's diamond jewelry, which probably was insured anyway.

Matt nodded, listened, didn't defend himself, thinking not of the jewelry but of the weapons he'd seen in the van, the reports he'd been hearing too often lately about teenagers and guns, and the way they used them, not as tools, but as machines for slaughter. He hadn't been protecting jewelry; he'd been protecting the smiling baby who had grabbed his spirit-gummed beard and tried to chew it; the little girl who had laughed with her father with such complete joy. He had been protecting the small throne and the Ella Fitzgerald Christmas carols, and the gray light coming in from the atrium windows.

He had done it without thinking, and now that he could think, he knew he would do it all over again.

The cops must have seen the determination on his face, for they tried to reassure him. He had done well; he would be a hero; the boys were in custody. The robbery fit a pattern that had started a few weeks before, and even though the robberies were brazen, no one had been able to catch the thieves. They might stop now, after a taste of prison, a taste of pain, one of the cops said, and laughed. The display case had probably broken the kid's pelvis, and no man ever forgot that.

Matt waited until they were done, was cordial and kind until they dismissed him, and then went to the locker room to put on his street clothes. For the first time since he had quit five years before, he longed for a cigarette. The destructive impulse made him sadder than it should have, and he wondered what it was about the night that inspired him to make things worse.

***

THAT NIGHT HE WOKE in a cold sweat, the smooth polished feel of a shotgun still heavy in his hands, the heat of the summer's day covering him, the sound of a woman's voice, pleading, still echoing in his ears. He sat up in his rented bed and blinked in the unfamiliar darkness, the dream slowly fading.

It wasn't a dream really: it was a memory as clear as if it had happened just that night. The tinkle of the bell over the convenience store's glass door, the sharp smell of cheap perfume and plastic, the way the clerk had looked at him—terror making her face rounder, her eyes bigger, her mouth a silly but perfect circle. He lifted his grandfather's shotgun to his shoulder and shot out the cameras—all of them a perfect bulls-eye—and then he had tugged his ski mask to make sure it was in place.

The clerk had screamed after each shot, and when he finally turned the gun on her—his foster father's voice echoing in his head *Don't point a gun at anyone unless you mean to use it*—she had started pleading for her life: a single run-on sentence filled with spit and panic.

Don'tshootmemisterreallyI'lldoanythingyouwanthone stbutjustpleasedon'tshootmepleasepleasedon'tshootme.

For five days he had cased the place, realized it was a mom-and-pop organization that didn't like to do bank runs. It had a safe in the back filled with the day's takings, probably fifteen hundred dollars, maybe more, a lot of money in 1984. He had planned carefully, wearing someone else's clothes, bought at a Goodwill fifteen miles away, boots three sizes too big, with a heel that made him seem inches taller. A wig beneath his ski mask, and a Southern accent, spoken in a voice lower than his usual.

Because she had been so terrified, because he hadn't expected that, because he realized at the moment he stared down his gun at her that they both knew he could kill her, he took the money. Then he ripped out the phone, and made her lie down, telling her to wait until he had been gone fifteen minutes before she went for help. He set a wind-up toy on the floor and let it shuffle around so that she would still think he was in the store, then he slipped out the back door, the manager's door. He had a car waiting around the block—stolen that afternoon off a car lot in the same town as the Goodwill. He'd hot-wired the car, and left it running, figuring if someone else took it on a joyride it would be no big deal, might even get him off the hook.

But it was there, waiting for him, its exhaust rising like fog in the streetlights. He got in, removed his mask and wig, placed them in a plastic bag, put the money with them, and drove the car back to the lot. He replaced the $800—*Like New!* sign, and walked away as if he had never taken the car. His truck was parked behind a library a mile away. He walked awkwardly in the big boots. When he got to the truck, he slid into the cab, removed the boots, changed clothes, and threw them in the plastic bag. Then he removed the money, put it in an envelope, and stuck it in the glove box. He put a brick in the bag and tied it closed.

He drove all night, and the next day, just before dawn, as he was about to cross the Ohio River in Evansville, he took a side road, found a bridge no one was near, and chucked the plastic bag over the side. Then he drove back to the main highway and crossed into Kentucky, a new man. A man who had had nerve. A man who had stolen from someone else.

A man he could have killed if his finger had slipped.

He kept the money for two days, spreading it on the seat of his truck, never counting it, wearing gloves every time he touched it despite the August heat. And finally, he realized he'd never be able to spend it or add to it, that for the rest of his life, he'd see the clerk's round face, her big eyes and her silly circle of mouth, and know that for a few thousand dollars, he had nearly taken her life.

In Cairo, he put the money in an envelope, and mailed it back to the convenience store—its address burned in his brain from his five days of study, the 152 painted in black above the door like a neon sign every time he closed his eyes. He drove on to Memphis and told his first real lie to get his first honest job, and never looked back.

He had thought it would be easy money. But he hadn't realized he was still paying for it, even now.

He wrapped his arms around his knees, felt the thin rubbery blanket beneath the flesh of his forearms, the industrial smell of the sheets tickling his nose. No one was looking for him. The clerk would remember. He did. And maybe the mom-and-pop owners thought of that one time they'd been robbed. But no one else did. The cops who had worked the case were probably long gone.

He watched the true-life mystery shows and all the real-life cop dramas and never once had he seen the brief image of his own body, standing in that convenience store, pointing his grandfather's shotgun at the camera.

Still, because of tonight's heroics, he toyed with packing his bags, getting into the new truck, the one he'd had for the last year, and heading down I-5. It was still early. Maybe they were hiring Santas in Eugene, or Roseburg, or even in California.

But he couldn't do that. He finally understood what kind of peace he had shattered that night so long ago. He finally understood that he had done more than point a gun at a woman, and break a few laws. He had violated something else, someone's dream, perhaps, or a woman's illusion of safety.

He had been a punk kid, whose parents had died when he was twelve, and whom his various foster parents believed was responsible enough to need very little supervision. A punk kid with a shotgun and an attitude who figured he didn't need to work for anything, that he was smarter than all the rest—hadn't he graduated straight A's in high school without doing any work? He'd figured criminals who got caught were the ones who hadn't paid attention to the details, and he was determined to make it rich by thinking.

Only he hadn't. He hadn't done any thinking at all.

Perhaps that burst of anger in the jewelry store hadn't been aimed at two teenage boys violating a mall with guns and a Santa bag. Maybe the anger had been at a single teenage boy who thought he could have the easy life by staking out a place, picking up a shotgun, and taking money from people who had spent long dirty hours earning it.

Maybe, just maybe, he had come a lot farther than he thought.

***

THE NEXT MORNING, he dressed early and stared at his bags, refusing to let himself pack them. He went to the mall on time, saw, as he got off the bus, the vans decorated with the logos of all the local news channels. Inside, a crowd of cameras studied Santa's Village, but didn't film the grandfather. Instead, they were waiting for Matt.

He hesitated. They didn't recognize him in his street clothes. He could turn around and leave, and no one would be the wiser. Then, of course, someone would investigate his résumé, realize that there was no Professor Sturtz at Gustavus Adolphus, and the entire story would turn bizarre in the space of an afternoon.

The jewelry store was open, the sole employee with the official rumpled look of a manager facing more stress than he expected. The damaged display had been placed behind the counter, but a cameraman was asking, rather loudly, that the display be moved back to its original location.

Matt bit his lower lip, then felt a hand on his arm. The mall manager smiled uncertainly at him, and said, "They want you in the Santa suit, if that's all right."

Matt nodded, then felt some of the tension leave his shoulders. Not that he was worried about being caught—whatever happened, happened—but because he was worried about ruining this moment for everyone else. Every now and then a mere mortal, dressed as Santa, did something spectacular. It helped the kids believe.

It brought a smile to the face of weary parents. It gave the season a shining layer of gold.

He changed into his suit, made an appearance, and let the cameras turn their shiny lenses on him, while the reporters asked questions, posed him in the scene of the crime, in the village, with a volunteer child. He smiled and laughed and waited patiently until it was all done, and when they finally left to find another human interest tale or to chase an ambulance, he winked at his elf—a different woman from the night before—and asked if she was ready to get back to business. She was.

The children filed through, the photos were snapped, gifts were given. He held each wriggling little body as if it were more precious than diamonds, and he made sure each little wish was passed on, just as he had before.

It had been this that had changed him, this small tradition, seeing how important it was to each child, each parent, waiting patiently in his line. It wasn't the deed that mattered so much as the life lived. His had been empty, purposely, except for this one tradition, this single month where he was at his best. Somehow that pushed him farther, made him do more than he ever thought he could.

He would still wander away from Portland, and Matt Sturtz would disappear forever. But there was an old name, nearly forgotten, a real name that could be dusted off, along with dreams and goals, and perhaps the person who owned that name could find a way of contributing more than a merry laugh, a few empty promises, and a jolly red suit.

He had a few weeks to think about how he would do that, what would be his best plan. And no matter what he actually did—whether he went back to that tiny Midwestern town and confessed or whether he found another way to pay for his sins—he knew, that when he gave the suit back, he wouldn't wait until next Thanksgiving to become the person he wanted to be. He wouldn't let the season fade. He would work at keeping the shine, every day of the coming year.

The Moorhead House

T HE HOUSE ON THE HILL had Christmas lights.

I stopped beside my van—white, with *DUSTY'S CLEANING* lettered in discreet gold. The van was camouflage—official enough, without advertising the kind of work I actually did—but people knew anyway. Hard to miss when the guy down the street offs himself, and a woman in a hazard suit, driving a van loaded with cleaning supplies, shows up a few days later.

But that day, I was alone. I was touring a cleaned scene, making sure my team had gotten every last bit. I wore my coveralls, a mask and three pairs of gloves, but I hadn't gone for the full treatment, thinking it unnecessary.

The neighborhood was solidly Oregon middle-class: old Victorians, 1930s bungalows, a few ranches; late-model cars, all probably bought on time; and lovely yards with only a little grass and lots of perennials. The kind of neighborhood a prospective buyer would look at and think of as a nice place to raise kids, the kind of place you grow old in, where your neighbors watch out for you, and keep track of every little thing.

But I'd been here four times in the ten years I'd owned this business—for the Hansen suicide (right in the living room, where the kids couldn't miss it. Bastard); the Palmer home-invasion-gone-wrong (the crime scene techs had missed the cat, curled up under the stove where it had apparently crawled to nurse its wounds); the well-known Bransted murder (the little girl had been dragged into a nearby garage and gutted there, mercifully after death); and the Moorhead ritual slaughter in the Victorian up the hill.

At least, the authorities believed it was a ritual slaughter. They never did find the bodies, although that place had four different high velocity spatters, and all sorts of ritualistic items—knives, black candles, destroyed crosses. That was the only case I'd ever been called to testify in, mostly because the members of that cult were convicted even though no one ever found the victims.

The murders had occurred over Christmas.

The first time I'd seen the Moorhead House, it'd been covered with Christmas lights like something out of a Hallmark greeting. All it needed had been two feet of snow, and a few carolers out front, holding their lanterns, their red-cheek faces upturned in wholesome rapturous praise.

My first partner'd quit after that job. Not that I blamed her. The Moorhead job had left me shaken too, and I'm not the shakable type. I'm a former firefighter and EMT, one of the first women in the state to do that kind of work, and I've battled both flame and discrimination with equal ferocity. I've seen what people can do to each other, and I've learned to accept it most of the time.

Since then, the Moorhead House had sold more than once, but no one had ever been able to live there long. So far as I knew, the place had been empty for years.

The Christmas lights bothered me.

They were up in the same place those original lights had been, white icicles—popular ten years ago—dripping down like melted frosting off the gables and the eaves of the Queen Anne.

So much like that dusky winter afternoon, when I'd seen the destruction for the first time.

Back then, I had no clue how to handle the destruction, the tears that cleaning a drop of blood from the back of a lamp might bring. I tried to pretend that I was just cleaning a place, a very filthy place, and I was beginning to realize that would never really function, that you couldn't stop the brain from wondering how it must've felt among the screams and the crashing and the glinting knife.

The state waited nearly a month before letting us in. By then, the place smelled like ancient rot and old blood.

That smell came back to me as I stared at those lights, promising a festive afternoon to anyone who would just march up the hill, and knock.

***

"Who's in the Moorhead House?" I asked when I got back to the office. "Office" is too big a word for the place: that makes it sound like we all have desks and secretaries and official nameplates. In reality, I have a tiny office and the rest of the place is two rooms—the front area with a desk, a phone, and a Coke machine that Debbie insisted on as well as a warehouse-style back room, filled with all manner of cleaning equipment, industrial strength showers, and five commercial washer and dryer sets.

Marcus sat behind the desk that afternoon. He's a big guy with a deep, reassuring voice, the kind folks like to hear when they've had a death in the family and decide to hire us themselves.

"Seen the lights, huh?" he said, leaning back in his chair and folding his massive hands over his surprisingly flat stomach.

"Yeah." I punched the Coke machine, and a root beer fell out.

We'd long ago bought the cola people out, filled the machine with our favorite cans, and shut off the payment mechanism. Now the thing works like an oversized (and expensive) refrigerator. I don't get rid of it though, because it's the only nifty part of our office.

"To be honest," I said, popping the top, "it scared me a little."

"Dwayne said that too."

I'd forgotten Dwayne worked the second part of that job—when the first set of new owners somehow got it into their heads that the tiny bones in the septic system belonged to the murdered family. The bones actually belonged to a family of squirrels. But by then, the crime scene techs had been back to the house and the lawn dug up. The mess was incredible, and the crime scene people decided to call us.

Not that it mattered to the first new owners. They sold as soon as the place was presentable again.

"How come that job weirded you out?" Marcus asked.

I shrugged, took a sip of the root beer, and said, "Sometimes I wonder why more jobs don't weird me out."

"Nice avoidance," he said. "Now answer."

I smiled at him. "Because there're no bodies."

"There're never any bodies when we go in," he said.

Which wasn't entirely true. There was that cat in the Palmer house and farther downtown, a stray dog left on the back porch. One of our other cleaning teams discovered an infant in a back closet, an infant which hadn't been part of the murder that the team had been cleaning up.

But I got Marcus's point. The bodies that we cleaned up after were long gone by the time we got to the house. We always knew what happened—we had to, so that we would know where to look for debris or spatter or pieces of skin—but we almost never saw the corpse.

"I think it would have been easier if there had been bodies." I set the root beer down. "It was the uncertainty."

Or maybe it had been my uncertainty. As an EMT, I'd pulled dying people out of car wrecks. As a firefighter, I'd been at houses where the children didn't get out, where the remaining person on the fifth floor refused to jump, where entire families died in their sleep.

But nothing prepared me for the emptiness of a crime scene. The moved furniture, the ruined rugs, the destroyed curtains. The toys that were pushed against the wall, the broken vases, the shattered lamps.

We couldn't repair that stuff. Our mission was to make sure no one could tell a violent or neglected death had happened in this place. And if the family still lived there, our mission was to make the place look like it had before what we euphemistically called, "The Event."

But the Moorhead House was the first place I worked without a family to move back into it or without an owner overseeing the job we did on the rental property.

No family left, no extended family leaving messages on my machine, no potential owners waiting to rebuild the place according to their new vision.

I tried not to look at the Moorhead House as I drove to my next job. It wasn't far away—another suicide, damn the holiday season—and from the back door of a kitchen that hadn't been cleaned since 1978, I could see the lights of the Moorhead House against the rain-darkened sky.

I tried to ignore it, to concentrate on the life lost, the loneliness that seemed to be the cause. This man hadn't been found for nearly two weeks, which put his death on Thanksgiving Day. The remains of a small turkey and the store-bought pumpkin pie confirmed that.

He had family—an estranged wife who hadn't seen him in nearly thirty years, two children now grown, and parents who sounded genuinely hurt when they hired us over the phone.

I'd learned, though, that genuine hurt sometimes sounded brusque or businesslike, not thick with tears.

And I wondered about a man whose house was so dirty that the neighbors didn't complain about the odor because they were used to odors coming from the place.

I never told my co-workers that I thought about the dead as if I were the last person who would remember them. Sometimes, perhaps, I was. Certainly the family of that man wouldn't know how bleak his life was at the end. Even if one of us told them, they wouldn't be able to imagine the piled up papers, the half-written letters, the battered but comfortable chair in front of the TV.

I recognized this house because it was a filthy version of my own.

My place is spotless. Because my hours are long and my moods uncertain, I don't keep a pet. I have the battered but comfortable single chair in front of a too-big television, only it's in my basement, not the center of the living room.

If someone asked me, I'd never admit to being lonely. Usually I don't mind.

Except on difficult days, days when I'm cleaning out someone else's solitary home.

***

THE INVITATION CAME TWO DAYS LATER. The city's annual bash, held for the contractors and private firms that kept the city running, was always a big deal. The planners spared no expense. Once they rented a yacht to follow the old ferry route across the river. Another time, they commandeered the largest, trendiest night-club in the city. And one time—the only time (because too many people complained)—they held a beautiful secular service at the city's historic Presbyterian Church.

This year, however. This year's site was a stunner.

Debbie handed me the invite not three minutes after the mail arrived. I was sitting in my office, enjoying a rare moment of quiet. I had that week's checks spread in front of me. I was thinking about the bank deposit, and having a healthy bank balance at the Christmas holidays for the first time since I'd opened the business.

"Boss," Debbie said.

I looked up. Her normally dusky skin had paled to an abnormal gray color. She held the invitation between her thumb and forefinger as if it smelled bad.

It didn't look bad. In fact, I recognized it. We usually didn't get formal invitations here, not the kind with the gold foil borders and the hand calligraphy.

"What's wrong?" I asked.

She handed me the invite. It was on a stiff cardboard stock that felt like expensive parchment. I glanced at the language, familiar with it after ten years of parties.

"The annual party," I said. "So?"

"Look where they're holding it."

I did. And felt the blood leave my face as well.

The Moorhead House.

"Get me the envelope," I said.

She went back to reception. I could see her through my door, rummaging through the wastebasket. When she finally found the envelope, she carried it back to me in the same way she had carried the invite itself—thumb and forefinger, as if the entire thing would infect her.

I took the envelope from her. It was made of a matching stock and had a metered city hall postmark from the day before. If someone had sent this as a joke, they would have had to duplicate the card stock and use the city hall postage meter, which gets guarded like crazy so that city hall employees don't use it for personal letters.

"Crap," I said, and reached for the phone.

I dialed the RSVP number at the bottom of the invite. After a few rings, I got the voice mail of a person I didn't know. I hung up, and dialed the deputy mayor, Greg Raabe. We had gone to college together. We'd even dated a few times before I had found my calling and before he had met his wife.

His secretary picked up immediately, and when she heard it was me, put me through even faster.

"Greg," I said without preamble, "what's this about the Christmas party at the Moorhead House? Do you remember what happened there?"

"I remember," he said, which was not the response I expected. I expected some political dance or an actual lapse of memory. The fact that he answered—and sounded disgusted—meant that he had fielded more than one call about this.

"Don't you think this is a little inappropriate?"

"What I think doesn't matter," he said. "It's a done deal."

"Why?" I asked.

"Because," he said, "the city bought the building. They plan to turn it into a museum."

***

THAT WAS THE THING about the Moorhead House, the thing no one talked about any more. Shortly after the family died, the National Register of Historic Places placed the house on its registry. Apparently someone had gone through the entire historic preservation rigmarole in the years before the murders.

Fortunately for me, the certification came after we cleaned the place up. If it had come before, the job would have taken much longer, and the city would have been billed for a great deal more money.

Historic preservation crime scene cleaning required an entirely different use of chemicals, several kinds of oversight, and all sorts of paperwork, things I'd just managed to avoid.

I'd managed to overlook most of that and had, in fact, forgotten it, until Greg Raabe had said the word "museum."

The Moorhead House had been the first home built on this side of the river. The fabulously wealthy Moorheads had made their money in various enterprises in the Oregon territory, from logging to mining to trading supplies. Then they bought up the land surrounding the river, and sold it, piecemeal, to settlers coming down the Oregon Trail.

The Moorheads kept large portions of the land, however, much of it near the river, so that they could control the ferries (the only way to get across and head to Portland, even then the state's major city). The river also gave them added control of the logging industry. In those days, logs floated down the river to be collected at sloughs which were also owned by the Moorheads. Over time, the river land became a center for what little industry the city had, and the rents made the Moorheads even wealthier.

But they became enchanted with their wealth, and wanted a lot more power than owning a single small city would give them. The great-grandsons of the original family moved to Portland, where they bought even grander houses on even grander hills. Their sons became politicians, and their children became drug-addicted deadbeats who had every privilege.

Somewhere along the way, the holdings here got sold. Then the houses in Portland went, and finally, the famous family, now down to an infamous few, had only enough left to maintain their townhouses in Washington D.C.

The Moorhead House, symbol of the wealth and power of a bygone age, had—even before the federal government decided to protect it—become the symbol of death and destruction in the modern age.

"A museum?" I asked.

"People love a mystery," Greg said in that dryly bland voice, the one I always thought of as his political voice. "And the house is truly historical. The museum will have one room dedicated to the murders, but it'll be upstairs.

The rest'll talk about city history, the impact of the Moorheads, and the way that this part of Oregon once seemed like the center of the universe."

Then I knew he was being sarcastic. He never used that phrase in serious conversation.

"Whose idea was this?" I asked.

"You read about it in the papers?" he asked as if that was an answer.

"No," I said.

"Then think about it."

I did, and it only took me a minute to understand. The mayor had done this. The mayor, Louise Vogel, had set herself up as a minor dictator, much to the disgust of everyone outside of her party and even some within.

She had the benefit of being one of the few people in the city who would take the job, which paid next to nothing for the amount of work it took. Greg had become deputy mayor as a sort of oversight position, but she had defanged him quickly. She owned much of the council, bought, I was told, with a combination of blood money and blackmail threats. The woman knew how to run small city politics.

"Why in the world would Louise want the Moorhead House as a museum?" I asked.

"I have no idea," Greg said. "Makes as much sense to me as holding a Christmas party there. So, are you coming?"

"I cleaned the place, Greg," I said softly. "I had to testify at the trial."

"Oh." He was silent for a moment. Then he sighed. "I'm supposed to jolly people into attending."

"Has it been working?"

"So far," he said. "Apparently, people like to pretend they're not interested in death houses, but they really are."

Unless they see the houses in full aftermath.

"I suppose it'll be a grand affair," I said, mimicking his dry voice.

"It'll be memorable, that's for sure," he said, and signed off.

I held onto the phone for a moment longer, mostly to fend off Debbie's questions. As she listened to my conversation, she seemed to have gotten ahold of herself. She shook her head and shifted from foot to foot, as if she could barely contain herself.

I set the receiver down. "It's no joke."

She swallowed. "Are we going?"

The city's party was always the highlight of our year.

"Greg says the party'll be memorable," I said.

"People will talk about it for a long time," she said.

I adjusted some of the checks in front of me. My pleasure in my unusual wealth at year's end had faded.

"Let's make attendance optional this year," I said. "And before anyone agrees to go, make sure they know that the party'll be at Moorhead House."

"Okay." Debbie started to leave my office, then she paused at the door. "You going?"

"I don't know," I said, and realized, to my surprise, that I had just spoken the truth.

***

I SUPPOSE, POLITICALLY, I should have said I was going to go. My job, after all, was to make buildings habitable again. Part of habitable was holding festive events—weddings, bar mitzvahs, Christmas parties.

But habitable was different than comfortable. And habitable wasn't always possible.

Places like Moorhead House were notorious, and notoriety lingered long after the physical examples of the crimes had disappeared.

In the end, it was my curiosity that took me there. I wanted to see the house in all its glory. I wanted to know if it could still have glory.

And I wanted to know exactly what Louise Vogel was up to this time.

***

NO ONE ELSE FROM THE OFFICE wanted to go. Debbie actually called me ghoulish, even though I wasn't the person holding the party. Dwayne looked at me with pity, asked me if I was sure, and when I said I was, he visibly shuddered. Then he told me, quietly, that he'd never go in that house again, not even if I paid him to do so.

In the end, Marcus went with me, mostly because he was curious. He'd been hired long after I did the first part of the Moorhead House job, but he was there for the tail end of the trial, and for Dwayne's run at the tiny bones in the sewers. Marcus told me he'd always wanted to go inside, and acknowledged that it was an unhealthy curiosity, based as much on the missing bodies as it was on the effect the entire place had had on our office.

He picked me up at eight. I'd forgotten how well he cleaned up. He wore a long jacket over dress pants—a modern suit that harked back to the Old West—and instead of looking like a football player stuffed into his younger brother's clothing, he looked like something out of *GQ*.

I felt dowdy in comparison. I wore a black velvet dress, and I decked it with a red scarf and some glittery (but fake) jewelry I'd inherited from my great aunt. My matching black velvet heels required, of all things, dusting, and I had to run out an hour before the party to buy panty hose without runs or pulls.

Marcus waited inside my foyer while I dithered over coats and purses, feeling more like a girl-girl than I had for awhile. Once upon a time, I had cared about things like make-up and matching purses with shoes, but I had lost that at nineteen, when I'd come home from college to find my mother dead of a stroke on the kitchen floor.

She had been there for a week. My parents were divorced—my father lived in another state—and I was an only child. I had come home to surprise my mother, and instead, she had surprised me.

Marcus had a 1960s Mustang that he took out for special occasions, and apparently this ranked as one of those. He drove to the Moorhead House in silence. Normally, we would have chattered the entire way—Marcus and I share the same taste in movies, books, and politics—but those subjects paled in comparison to the house.

The Mustang rode lower than my van, so the view of the Moorhead House as we turned onto the street below seemed even more impressive that usual. This close to Christmas, you'd think other homes on the block would have decorations on the windows or lights strung outside, but the Moorhead House seemed to be the only one with Christmas spirit.

I looked up at the place as we started toward the drive, and those icicle lights still sent a chill through me. I almost told Marcus to turn around and I'd buy him dinner at a nearby steakhouse so we wouldn't waste the dress-up clothes, but I didn't. I knew better than to seem weak in front of one of my employees.

I'd learned that lesson as a female fire-fighter. Even when you felt uncomfortable, you took a deep breath and went into the smoke. To do anything less meant you couldn't perform your duties.

And somehow, this party had become one of my duties.

***

WE WERE ARRIVING DELIBERATELY LATE. I hated showing up early to any party. Marcus pulled the Mustang into the circular drive, and my breath caught.

Some things were different: the hedges had been clipped to the bone and did not have lights hanging from them as they had that murderous Christmas season. Signs had been planted in what had been the yard but was now obviously going to be a garden, warning guests to stay on the paths. The signs had been hand-calligraphed, and looked expensive. They even had little drawings of holly around the edges.

I hated them.

Marcus looked at me as he got out of the Mustang, and then he grinned like a little boy who was about to do something wrong.

"Ready, boss?" he asked.

I'd never be ready, but I smiled gamely and put my hand on his massive arm. He helped me pick my way across the path. The air was cold and damp, but the pine boughs near the house gave off a Christmasy scent that I hadn't expected.

Suddenly I felt younger than I had in years, almost like that girl I'd left in my mother's kitchen, and my heart lifted. A party was just what I needed. If I could forget the house, or at least look on its new role as host as a personal victory, I might be able to have a good time.

We stepped onto the porch together. Inside the frosted glass windows, we could see shapes moving against yellow light.

My stomach clenched, and I swallowed convulsively.

I wasn't sure I could do this.

Marcus gave me a sideways glance. "You okay?"

I nodded because I couldn't answer. He knocked on the door.

Someone pulled it open and the smells of burning wood and baking cookies filled the air. Laughter came along with Mel Tormé's voice, singing about Jack Frost nipping at noses. The man who opened the door had a Santa hat over graying hair. The hat didn't go with his exquisitely tailored suit.

He held a glass clearly filled with eggnog in one hand. With the other, he gestured toward the interior. "Merry, merry!"

"Happy, happy," Marcus said, making fun of him.

But the man didn't seem to notice. He clapped Marcus on the back as we walked inside.

The place was transformed. If I hadn't known it was the house in which I'd spent a week cleaning, I wouldn't have recognized it. To my right, the curved staircase was once again the center of the house. Someone had wrapped garlands of holly around the mahogany banister, probably with no thought to how old, how rare or how valuable the wood was.

People stood on the stairs, holding drinks, talking, some looking at the portraits hung over the stairs, others heading up to see what else the house had in store.

Coats were piled on top of the telephone seat built against the wall. The carpets were gone, revealing wood floors that matched the wood trim throughout the house.

I couldn't imagine what it had cost to clean the floors. I had cleaned the carpets and recommended their removal, but no one had done that—at least not for the first family which bought the place. I had warned the realtors that if anyone took up the carpets, they might find horrible stains beneath. I had removed the rugs myself in the upstairs bedroom where two of the family members had bled to death (there was no saving those rugs, and no attempt to), but the ones down here had had bloody footprints and drag marks, and other stains that I never could quite identify.

"You're staring," Marcus whispered.

At least, I thought he whispered it, although he might have spoken in a normal tone. The party noises going on around us made it hard to hear much more than the rumble of conversation. The music was classy and so were the people around me. Hard to believe most of them spent their days in jeans and overalls or uniforms paid for by the city.

"Sorry," I whispered.

"Is it different?" he asked.

"Yeah."

I led Marcus into what had once been the front parlor. The pocket doors were gone, along with most of the walls that contained them, so now the front and back parlors were one room (with an arch) that modern people would call the living room.

The furniture was fake period with a fainting couch, a regular couch, and overstuffed armchairs. Too many tables crowded the bay window, and on those tables stood food of all sorts from cookies and sliced pies to small unidentifiable appetizers and toothpicked bits of fruit and cheese.

Marcus grabbed a small plate, shaking it with surprise. "China."

"Nothing but the best," I muttered, and doubted he could hear me.

I couldn't eat, even if I wanted to. I left him there, debating whether to have strawberries dipped in chocolate or chocolate-covered cherry truffles. From a passing waiter carrying a tray of beverages on his outstretched palm, I snatched a flute of champagne, carrying it with me as I went from room to room.

The place had clearly been professionally decorated. From the furniture to the draped pine boughs and hanging mistletoe, the interior looked like something out of *House Beautiful*.

The Christmas tree, at the far wall of what had been the back parlor, took up so much space that it seemed to be growing out of the floor. It was decorated in silver bows, tinsel, and little silver lights that blinked on and off. An embarrassing display of packages hid the lower branches.

I knew from previous parties that the packages would be gone by the night's end, a mound of paper left for someone else to clean up, and the gifts would seem less impressive unwrapped than they did at this moment.

A *Do-Not-Enter* sign had been taped to the swinging kitchen door, the only infelicity in the entire place. I ignored it, and went inside anyway, drawn by the smells of baking cookies. Small women in rented tuxedos and looking hot, wiped hair away from their faces. Two coaxed a stainless steel dishwasher to take more dishes. Another woman bent over the stove, and yet another was placing crudités on a silver tray.

Men, as tall as the women were small, picked up the trays. The men also wore tuxes, but on them, the tuxes looked natural. Maybe because they were in traditional serving roles, where the women, stuck in the kitchen, should have been in simple black dresses with aprons to complete the servant illusion.

"You're not supposed to be here," said the woman filling the trays.

"That's all right," I said. "I used to work here."

One of the men looked at me sharply. He frowned a little, as if wondering how anyone could have worked here, given the history of the house. Or maybe I was reading too much into a slight reaction. Maybe he thought my lame excuse for being in the kitchen was just that. I smiled at him, and slipped out of the way.

The kitchen was dramatically different, remodeled about the time of the bones discovered in the sewer drain. The stove was restaurant quality, the refrigerator one of those stainless steel subzero monstrosities that looked like it could eat an entire room.

Everything was different, and somehow I found that more disconcerting than the Christmas decorations around front. When I had cleaned this place, the kitchen had been my haven—the only room without much blood in the entire house, and that blood only came from the detectives and crime scene techs. Harmless, innocuous drops, left by people who were trying to solve the crime, not the people who had created it.

My stomach was churning. The smell of food was making me ill. I pushed open the swinging door and stepped back into the living room.

Marcus was talking to a pretty woman in a slinky blue dress. Louise was standing near the tree, gesturing at the presents. She looked even thinner than usual, her face bony, her black hair pulled into a tight bun.

Her gaze caught mine, flat and challenging. I lifted my still full glass in a silent toast. She smiled—a real and warm smile, something I had never seen from her before—and raised her glass as well. We drank in concert from separate parts of the room as if we were old friends.

"I see you've kissed and made up." Greg Raabe, the deputy mayor who had told me about this debacle, had sidled up beside me. He knew how much I disliked Louise, and how that feeling seemed to be mutual.

I turned to him and smiled. He no longer looked like the boy I'd dated in school. That boy had been reedy slender and blond, with no muscles at all. His bright blue eyes had dominated his face.

The eyes remained the same, dominating and filled with personality, but the rest of him had changed. He was as heavy as he had once been slight, and in place of those visible ribs were rock-hard abs from all the weights he lifted. He ate to compensate for the tension, I think, because he didn't drink or smoke, and to compensate for the eating, he exercised.

"There was no kissing," I said to him, happier than I wanted to be to see him. "I just saluted her, that's all. This is quite the party."

"This is quite the expense," he said. "Imagine what the council will say when they see this on the city budget."

I grinned. "Fortunately, that's not my job."

"But it could be mine," he said, looking at her talking to the man near the presents. "I was kind of hoping that once she had her stepping stone to the governorship, I could become mayor."

"One party won't get in the way," I said.

"You're assuming that this party is the only budget item that'll bother them." He sighed and grabbed his own champagne flute from a passing waiter.

I looked up at the waiter as he went by. It was the man who had frowned in the kitchen. He looked familiar. His skin was a ruddy color that wasn't common in the Pacific Northwest, except among people who worked on the ocean. He had a square jaw, and hard cheekbones, the kind I always associated with those 1930s pictures of Aryan youth.

"Know him?" Greg asked.

"He looks familiar," I said as he went into the kitchen. "Does he to you?"

"In a generic waiterly way." Greg smiled. "I told Louise we should have dancing, but she didn't listen to me."

"There's no room," I said. Besides, Greg wouldn't have been able to dance with me even if there had been music. His wife Emma pretended that the fact we dated didn't bother her, when, in fact, it was very clear that it did.

I scanned the room, but didn't see her. "Is Emma upstairs?"

The smile left his face. "She wouldn't come."

"Because of the house?" I asked.

"Because of the separation." His voice was low. "She doesn't like my ambitions."

Emma had always wanted Greg to settle down and make money. He had always been more interested in public service than in making monetary use of his expensive law degree. Apparently the fights had come to a head.

"When did you separate?" I asked.

He shushed me and whispered. "Not everyone knows."

"Sorry," I said.

"It happened last week. I have an apartment near city hall, which I'd had anyway. I guess I knew this was coming."

Everyone had known this was coming, maybe even from the moment the vows were taken. But Greg seemed quietly devastated.

I put my hand on his shoulder, startled to feel the same kind of muscles I had felt on Marcus. "I'm really sorry," I said again.

Greg grinned. The look didn't quite meet his eyes. "No, you're not. You never liked Emma."

Not many of his friends had, and I always figured the ones who had liked her just pretended for Greg's sake.

"I am sorry," I said. "For you. This is hard."

"Yeah," he said, and then sighed. "Duty beckons."

Duty didn't, but Louise did. She was waving him over with a hand so manicured I could see the shine of the nail polish from here. Time for the packages. I hoped they got to my name quickly. I was ready to leave.

Marcus had left his new conquest and came over beside me. "Did you check the upstairs?"

I shook my head. I hadn't forgotten the upstairs, but I didn't see the need to torture myself. "I ducked into the kitchen for a while."

Which reminded me of the waiter, whom I no longer saw. "Did you notice that waiter, the one who looked like he'd been a member of the Hitler Youth?"

"No," Marcus said. "Why?"

Greg had clapped his hands for quiet. I sighed. I knew this drill. First they'd demand silence, then they'd hand out gifts. Louise worked off a list. I had noted last year that the city contractors like me got one of two things: an espresso maker (if the city had spent a lot of money on you) or a care basket filled with all kinds of city products, like salmon and some of our famous cheese and locally grown filberts.

I, of course, had gotten a care basket, even though the city spent a lot of money on our services. I thought that it was merely an oversight, then Greg had reminded me that we weren't listed in the budget. We were buried in other line items. So no one really knew how much money we made cleaning up local property except maybe Debbie and me.

Greg started calling out names. The man beside Louise handed out the packages, and Louise kept charge of the list. People walked up, got large gaudily wrapped gifts, and then walked away, grinning.

Marcus rolled his eyes. "How long is this going to take?"

"Usually about an hour," I said. "You want to go back and make goo-goo eyes at that sweet young thing?"

"She's hard to talk to," he said.

"Because?" I asked.

His face shut down. "Because I told her what I do."

That was one of the major drawbacks to our business. People thought we were on the level of grave diggers and morticians. Even the popularity of programs like *CSI*, which made one small aspect of death work glamorous, didn't spill over to us.

"Tough break," I said.

He shrugged. "Anyone with reactions like that's too shallow for me."

But he didn't sound sincere. And then he took my champagne and finished it for me. I watched him drink another, and decided that at some point in the evening, I'd have to wrestle the Mustang's keys from him, and get us home.

***

It took two more hours before we could leave. I never did see the waiter again, but I got absorbed in my present—a small wireless weather forecasting kit, with barometer and thermometer, something that actually appealed to my scientific sensibilities. Marcus slowed on the drinks—he'd found another pretty woman to chat up, and apparently this time, he didn't make the mistake of telling her what he did—and I didn't want to interrupt his rhythm.

I looked at the stairs twice, but I didn't go up them. I searched for Greg, and found Louise instead. She was leaning against a side of the arch, holding but not drinking a glass of champagne. She watched the proceeding with tired eyes.

When she saw me, she smiled again.

I wasn't sure I liked that. Two real smiles from Louise in one evening. Something had to be wrong.

"It's going well, isn't it?" she asked.

"Better than I would have thought," I said.

She sipped the champagne—or pretended to. Maybe that was one of her secrets. Pretending to drink when everyone around her got blotto.

"It's a tribute to you people," she said.

At first, I thought she meant the little people, the non-politicos, and then I realized she actually meant us, Dusty's Cleaning.

"Thanks," I said, glancing at those stairs.

"I mean it," she said. "This place is cheerful. Who would have thought?"

I looked at her. Her entire face looked tired, and she was too thin. Maybe it was the strain of the party, or maybe something else had gone wrong in her life. I wasn't sure, and I wasn't about to ask.

"It's what we do," I said.

"Exorcise the ghosts," she said, as if in agreement.

But the ghosts weren't exorcised for me. They still lurked beneath the party favors and the seasonal joy. When this crowd left, and the caterers finished, when the last staff member shut off the lights, the house would revert to its post-murder self. The high-velocity spatter would paint itself on the walls, the cries would echo in the upstairs bedroom, and the blood would seep into the rugs.

I shuddered. I couldn't help it.

Of course, Louise noticed. "Does it still bother you?"

"Sometimes," I said before I could stop myself, "I think places like this should be burned."

Louise frowned at me. "That's an odd sentiment, coming from you."

I shrugged. "There are some places," I said, "that never get entirely clean."

***

THE DREAM CAME AS IT OFTEN DID. It started with my mother. She was on the floor of our kitchen, the smell of Lemon Pledge filling the air. When she saw me, she stood, apologized, and offered to cook. I thought it inappropriate to have the newly dead make the meal, and I told her so, even though I knew I was disappointing her.

She slipped out the side door, and as she did, she said, "You'll never see me again."

Only as I mulled the words, I realized she hadn't said "see," she had said "find." *You'll never find me again.*

Then, in the transitionless magic of dreams, I stood in the foyer of the Moorhead House. The place smelled of weeks-old blood and voided bowels. Beneath those smells was that of rotted flesh.

As I stood there, I existed on two levels: the woman standing in the foyer, and the woman who knew every inch of that house, the one who had cleaned it all and who would, if she wasn't careful, become obsessed with it.

The walls in the upstairs bedroom had a spatter pattern that looked like a post-modernist painting. I knew that it was spray—a knife or something sharp pierced an artery, and the blood sprayed before the dying man? woman? child? turned so that the rest of the blood would shoot against a different wall.

Then the dream changed. The waiter stared at me with those cold blue eyes. I'd seen them before. Not at a party where he was curiously out of place but at the trial.

He sat in the second row from the back, and watched my every move. His face wasn't ruddy then, but he was thinner, sadder, and his eyes had fear in them.

I couldn't look at him as I testified. He made me nervous.

That day, everyone made me nervous.

I thought nothing of it.

You'll never find me again.

Then the scene changed once more. My mother's kitchen, without her body lying on the middle of the floor, looked like a happy place—painted yellow, spotlessly clean. Only a chair had moved, tilted away from the table, as if its occupant left suddenly.

Add the body to the picture, sprawled along the tile, arms thrown backward, fluids staining the clothes, and the moved chair was ominous. Had she stood because she felt ill? Or had she simply been crossing to the refrigerator when her body gave out?

Or had she been laying there, helpless, only able to slide a chair a little toward her, thinking maybe it would help her up, but the experiment didn't work, and she remained—alone—on her back, until she breathed her last.

I sat up, not sure exactly when I woke, when the dream ended and the thinking began.

We could guess about the bodies in the Moorhead House, but we didn't know. We didn't know if the ritual items—the desecrated religious symbols, the black candles, the knives—had been added later to throw us off. Because they had been removed as evidence before I arrived, I didn't even know if they'd been covered with spatter, proving they'd been in position before the family died.

I did know that they left no impression wherever they'd been. There were no knife-sized holes in the spatter pattern, no black candle wax on the side tables.

Only the blood and the stink and the sense that something horrible had happened here.

I turned on my too-large television. One of the get-rich-quick real estate gurus hawked his no-money down method. As house after house flashed on the screen, I wondered what secrets those houses held.

Over time, the secrets faded.

All bodies disappeared, forgotten, lost.

Did the people who owned my mother's house now enjoy their kitchen? Did they walk easily over the spot where she had spent her last hours? Did they wonder how long her body had been there, waiting for someone to find her?

More importantly, did they care?

And that's when my stomach turned, when the crazy food that I had eaten backed up into my throat.

No one had cared at the Moorhead House party. If the murders were mentioned, it was with a salacious edge, as if the deaths were part of a setting, added for the party-goers' enjoyment.

Five people were missing, presumed dead—presumed because no one lost that much blood and lived.

But the police hadn't tested every drop. Only a few to make DNA comparisons, enough to build a case without a body—one of the toughest murder cases to bring. The cult, arrested, charged, and pulled off the street for life, had continually maintained their innocence.

I hadn't been able to look at them either when I testified—malnourished, scared twenty-somethings who'd used too many drugs and lived too close to the crime scene.

People had seen them in the house, but no one had seen them on the night of the murders.

No one had seen anything that night, even though the house dominated that hillside.

Even though the house dominated the entire town.

***

THE NEXT MORNING, we had a fire-clean. Mostly smoke and water damage. The apartment, on the lower floor of a large complex, had lost its kitchen, and the rest was ruined. But the upper floors were still livable if we could get the stench out, which we could.

The apartments had been evacuated, but they still held the stuff of people's lives—dolls scattered on a bedroom floor, slippers kicked aside in someone's haste to escape, a half-eaten pizza on a scarred coffee table.

I surveyed the damage, realized the cleaning would be one of our easier jobs, and called in a junior team. Then I went back to the office, and pulled the Moorhead files.

The image of my mother's kitchen chair, fresh from my dream, haunted me. We had approached the Moorhead scene with a single assumption: that the family had been slaughtered there in a ritualistic way, and the bodies had then been moved.

But what if there had been no ritual? What if this had been a crime of passion? Blood was everywhere in that house, except the kitchen, an oddity explained at the time by the ritualistic nature of the deaths.

I didn't have crime scene photos, but I did have my photos of the scene. It was the early days of my business; I did before-and-after photos for prospective clients.

The before photos were vicious and dark, grimmer than I remembered. But the blood spatter, the filth left from violent death, was much as my memory held it—a long, continuous spray, followed by real spatter, arcing as the blood pulsed from someone's body.

In one photo, my hand pressed on the rug, releasing the blood contained within. In another, the rivulets of blood went down the stairs, drops alongside heading away from the scene.

What had the police tested? What had they ignored?

I thumbed through until I found the bathrooms. They, like the bedrooms, were thick with blood. The toilet, the bathtub, and the sinks had light spray, but nothing inside the porcelain basins, suggesting that no one had cleaned up there.

No one had cleaned in the kitchen either.

I stared at the images, trying to recall the lesson of the dream. Take away my expectations, and what did I see?

A charnel house.

A place where blood was allowed to flow freely and for some time.

I closed the file and leaned on it, my stomach as queasy as it had been the night before. I rubbed my eyes, sighed heavily, and picked up the phone.

***

I HAD A LOT OF CONTACTS at the police department. Early on, they had considered me part of the brotherhood, mostly because of my EMT and fire training, and they handed out my cards to grieving widows and distraught adult children.

Over time, several officers would call me before the city did, letting me know I had a job on the way, and preparing me, so that I could put the proper team on it. If the case was sensitive, I often did the work myself. That way, if I found overlooked or lost evidence, I knew that it would be handled correctly. Mostly, I would leave it alone, and place a call on my cell. The forensic teams would arrive quickly because, I'd learned, it was me. My assistants often didn't get the same kind of respect.

Still, asking to see files in a case that had been closed for years was a sensitive thing. It irked all of us involved that we hadn't found the bodies, but, we had consoled ourselves, we had found the killers. I had taken this case as personally as the detectives who had worked it, and we all confessed late one night in the local cop bar that this was the case that haunted us.

Detective Jeffrey Foreno was the only one who had ever expressed doubts about the case. He had openly questioned whether the cult had done the killings. After all, he said, no blood was found in their hidey hole. No knives, no black candles. And nothing suggested they had been on the property that night. It had all been supposition and circumstance, fear and small-town politics.

He had been shushed pretty quickly.

So he was the one I went to that morning.

He was approaching retirement. The lines in his face were deep and grooved, accented by the white stubble he'd forgotten to shave off before coming to work. The rest of his hair was black and thick, in need of a cut. His eyes, once sharp and alert, were blood-shot, and when he saw me, he sighed.

"I knew someone would want to resurrect the dead." He leaned back in his chair, his hands folded over his stomach. "Just didn't expect it to be you."

I'd told him once I dreamed about cleaning the house, about the way the blood came back, as if the walls never wanted to give it up. He'd told me that he dreamed of the case too—of the Christmas tree that hadn't existed even though the outside of the house had been exquisitely decorated, of the lack of food in the kitchen, of the empty pet bowls, cleaned and stored in a dusty pantry.

"Why did you think someone would bring up the case?" I asked, sitting across from him.

He gave me one of those sideways looks that always made me nervous. Even with blood-shot eyes, Jeffrey Foreno had a way of looking all the way to your soul.

"The party," I said.

He pointed at me which, in Jeff language meant *You got it in one.*

"How come you didn't go?" I asked.

"It felt like dancing on someone's grave." Then he gave me that look again and his lips thinned. "You went."

I nodded. "Figured I had to. It had been my job to make sure no one noticed what had happened there."

He didn't move nor did his expression change. "Did it work?"

I shrugged. "I think Louise was using the murders to give the place ambience."

"The power of rubbernecking," he said.

"Yeah." I wouldn't have put it so crassly, but he was right. Maybe that was why I hadn't gone upstairs, why I refused to look at the rooms where the police had assumed most of the killings had taken place. Downstairs, the tree, the presents, the food, masked the prurience that went into the planning. Upstairs, the unvarnished truth—the naked interest on the hands of people more fortunate than the dwellers of the Moorhead House— would have been readily apparent.

"Did it open old wounds?" he asked.

I shook my head quickly, not sure I wanted to examine my answer to that question too closely.

"So you just came today out of curiosity," he said as if he didn't believe it.

"I came because I saw someone." I told him about the waiter, the way the man had looked at me, both at the party and at the courthouse.

Foreno shrugged. "Maybe he was one of the rubber-neckers. Some people make certain murder cases into their hobby."

"I know," I said. "But sometimes there's more to it."

He frowned at me.

"Remember anyone involved in the case who looked like that?"

"Like a perfect World War II German? Can't say as I do."

Put that way, I wouldn't have recognized him either. "I'd like to look through the file."

"Be my guest," Fareno said. "It's not going to bother anyone. Unless you find something."

We grinned at each other. Then he led me to records, got me the closed case files, and signed off so that I could work.

***

THE MOORHEAD FILE TOOK UP FIVE BOXES, most of them police and evidence reports. I gave the evidence reports a cursory glance, and saw exactly what I suspected: the assumptions began with the murder of the family and went from there. Most of the blood evidence was scraped from the wall of the bedroom—the crime scene tech's reasoning was simple: he didn't want to deal with the inevitable carpet fibers in the blood pool. Although, to his credit, he did cut carpet swatches as well, and stored them in one of the refrigeration units at the crime lab. Unless someone needed the space, the evidence might still be there.

I searched through the boxes until I found what I was looking for. Pictures. Not of the house, but of the family.

Five members—husband, wife, three children, the oldest being fifteen, the youngest twelve. Speculation by the investigating officer was that one or all of the children had had contact with the cult.

I stared at the father. His face was bony and Aryan too, almost but not quite the same as the waiter I had seen. The eldest son, fourteen, looked like his father or might have if he lived. That heavy bone structure was unusual, at least in these parts. I thumbed through the documents to see if there were other family members in the vicinity.

No one had located any. Pages and pages of police interviews, with neighbors, co-workers, friends, did not include anyone from the family.

Then I looked at the mug shots of the cult members. I remembered those faces from the trial as well. Young, confused, ravaged, they made me wonder whether those kids were vulnerable because they were following the wrong leader or whether they had followed the wrong leader because they were vulnerable.

I closed the boxes, feeling more uncertain than I had before I started. I put them back, and went upstairs to say good-bye to Foreno.

"Find anything?" he asked.

I shook my head.

"Let it rest." Then he gave me that look. "You're not going to, are you?"

"Who inherited the house?" I asked.

"No one," he said. "The state ended up with it."

"No family," I said.

"None that we could find." He tapped a pen against the top of his desk. "And before you ask, let me tell you I remember this because it seemed so damn odd. Two middle-aged parents with no family at all. No one remembered any grandparents or aunts and uncles visiting the kids. These people were an island."

"Their money went to the state too?"

"Eventually," he said. "Not that there was much of it."

"In a house like that?"

"Mortgaged and credit cards. The furniture wasn't even worth anything. The appearance of money, but no real money."

"Don't you find that strange?"

"Always have," he said.

"The guy I saw," I said, "looks a lot like the father."

Foreno cursed, then leaned back in his chair. "You sure?"

"It's not him," I said. "There're differences."

"Family differences?"

"I'd've thought they were brothers or cousins," I said.

Foreno frowned. Then he reached to the left and opened his bottom desk drawer. From my vantage, standing, I could see a dozen accordion files, all filled with manila folders. He thumbed through the files, then pulled out one folder.

He slid it to me, and stood.

"You want some lunch?" he asked. "I'm buying."

I looked at him with surprise.

He nodded toward a chair in the corner. "It'll take you a while to go through that."

"A sandwich would be nice," I said.

He grabbed his suit coat, then headed out the door. As he left, he pulled the door closed, so that someone passing by wouldn't be able to see me.

I found that curious, but not as curious as the file. It was thick with newspaper clippings and computer print-outs, some more than a decade old.

Cult killings, ritual murders, and bodiless cases. This was Foreno's comparison file. He was right: it took me quite a bit of time to read it. He managed to return with the sandwiches and we ate in silence while I read about beheadings and disembowelings, about corpses left in pieces all over property, about candles and black magic and pagan ceremonies.

In each, the bodies remained.

"You don't think they did it," I said, as I tossed my sandwich wrapper into the nearby trash.

"The cult?" He shook his head. "No, I don't think so."

"But the evidence points to them."

"Rather neatly," he said.

"So why didn't you speak up?"

"Because I had no other theory of the case," he said.

"Do you now?" I asked.

"Does your friend work for the catering firm?" And I realized he meant the man with the angular face.

"I think so."

"I'll see if I can track him down."

"And if you do?"

Foreno shrugged. "I'll see what happens next."

***

I WENT BACK TO WORK, thinking about all that blood, all those trails. The carpets were saturated, yet there were no footprints on the hardwood floors, no evidence of someone leaving through the front or back doors. The floors had been well-scrubbed with bleach, and one of the things I testified about was the way that bleach hid all evidence, one of the few things that masked even the goriest scene.

Why, the defense attorney had wanted to know, *would someone remove the footprints, but leave the blood droplets? Why leave the drag marks on the carpet uncleaned?*

I had shrugged. *People aren't that thorough. They clean only what they believe needs cleaning.*

Blood is blood, isn't it? he had asked, implying that someone who cleaned footprints on the hardwood would clean it all.

It's not that simple, I said. *I've had employees who missed spatter on their first few jobs because the scene was too overwhelming.*

Do you think the killer would be overwhelmed? The defense attorney had asked, but the prosecutor had objected to the question. I never got to answer.

Would the killer have been overwhelmed? I considered the question now, at the safety of my desk. Probably not. After all, he created the scene.

Three saturated carpets. Five dead humans. Six quarts of blood per body. That house was soaked, the scene an example—the prosecutor had said—of overkill.

We see what we want to see.

I went back to my notes and, for the first time, did the math.

***

THERE WAS TOO MUCH BLOOD. None of us had realized it. At least twice the amount that should have been in that house. Twice the deaths? Or had someone taken buckets of blood and poured it on the carpets, letting the liquid soak in after he had expertly sprayed the walls.

Reproducing crime scenes wasn't hard. Hollywood did it all the time, and there were photos of other scenes everywhere from forensic journals to true crime novels. Spatter and spray would be easy to reproduce—plant misters, set just right, would mimic the early parts of spray, and something with a bit of kick would be able to reproduce the way that blood spurted from an artery.

There'd be mistakes, but who would look for them? Especially in an overwhelming and fairly obvious scene.

Too much blood wasn't enough for Foreno to reopen the case—it was a closed murder trial, after all. But the blood evidence, coupled with the young man I'd seen, was enough to get Foreno working it again, on the side, in his spare time.

First, he had a crime scene friend re-examine the photos, not explaining anything about the case.

Second, he looked in the Moorhead family background.

Third, he searched for the waiter.

And those three things came together into something both expected and unexpected. The tech said the scene might've been tampered with. Impossible to know

now, although the blood was suspicious. Maybe someone else died.

The Moorheads traveled. They were running from debt in Michigan and used charm as well as the co-signature of an old friend to secure the house, which then got them credit cards and a new future.

Until the bank was ready to foreclose. Until the credit card companies had cut them off.

And the co-signer? The same man who had waited tables that night. The one who had overseen the court case. He was living under an alias, one he'd established twenty years before after he had embezzled fifty thousand dollars from a bank in the Midwest.

The bank where his brother had once worked.

The waiter wouldn't talk to the police—hiring a lawyer immediately—but his presence was enough to get those carpet samples tested.

Still refrigerated, still intact after all these years. Sometimes laziness was its own reward.

And that, Foreno said when he came to my office in May, was when it got interesting. The blood was all the same type—O Positive—but that was all it had in common. DNA testing proved that the blood came from dozens of sources, none of them related to the so-called victims.

Just the blood on the wall came from the family and, judging by the overlap in one of the bedrooms, had been applied just like I mentioned, with a sprayer and a lot of determination.

"Why?" I asked. "Why not just disappear? These people were smart enough to create new identities once before."

And that was when he showed me the police files. He'd actually made copies for me so that I could look at them.

Pages and pages and pages of complaints filed by the family, about the neighbors, about the young people in the house at the foot of the hill, about the parties and the goings-on, about the fears of devil worship and a possible cult.

Foreno shook his head. "Looks to me like pure old-fashioned hatred."

"For their neighbors?"

"Their young, unusual, and loud neighbors," Foreno said.

"They set these kids up?" I asked, and felt a shock at myself. I was willing to believe that a cult could off an entire family; I was not willing to believe that a family would set up innocent people in a way that might send them to jail for life.

"Looks like it," he said. "We've got work to do. They've got ten years and a lot of thinking on us."

"But you'll find them," I said.

"I hope so," he said. "But in life, there are no guarantees."

***

EXCEPT ONE.

The story leaked, and the leak coincided with the release of the annual budget. The party, the plans for the museum, and the cost to the taxpayer made page one of our usually sleepy rag.

For a while, it looked like Louise might implode because of the scandal. Then she hit on the right note: the case wouldn't be reopened—innocent people wouldn't be getting out of jail—if she hadn't been interested in the house in the first place.

She had a point, one I didn't care to think about.

Then one afternoon shortly after Halloween, I had to go to the Moorhead House for the final time.

***

I WENT WITH VARIOUS ATTORNEYS—the D.A., several assistants, and defense attorneys for a variety of clients from the waiter to the cult. Someone had found the youngest son in Miami, but he hadn't given up the rest of his family. His very presence—alive—in another state was enough to place doubt on the entire cult-killings story.

He wasn't represented by an attorney, so far as I knew, but I didn't ask a lot of questions.

Instead, I answered them, explaining what chemicals I used, defending myself and why I hadn't noticed the irregularities in the spatter, the extra blood, the lack of footprints.

Over and over again, I said simply that it wasn't my job.

And it wasn't. I was supposed to clean, not think. I was supposed to make the place livable again, and I had.

I had done everything I'd contracted to do.

Maybe that was why the house had haunted me so. Why I had dreamed of it, why the blood kept reappearing on the walls—not as if it couldn't be buried, but as if there was too much of it to contain.

My subconscious had known.

My conscious had refused to accept anything but what it had been told: a family had been murdered by their neighbors, a murderous cult, and the bodies hidden.

Differing interpretations of the same evidence—evidence not examined closely by any of us.

Except the brother, who had made two mistakes. First, he had come to the trial—nervously and obsessively worrying—to see if anyone had found the planted evidence. Or maybe he was stunned and appalled that a case with no bodies generated enough evidence for a conviction. Maybe the family had merely meant to harass the cult, not destroy their lives.

Then he had come back to the house, deliberately getting hired, just so he could see the site of his—and his family's—triumph. Or maybe he had still been worried, still afraid that he would get caught. Maybe he was guarding the place, hoping that no one figured it out.

Or maybe he simply couldn't stay away.

Like I couldn't.

I take evidence of a hideous event and make it vanish. I call that healing, but really, it's just masking. The event remains. It is history; it has happened. I allow people to pretend everything is all right.

What happened in the Moorhead House that day was the opposite of what I do. That family had used a masking technique to get revenge on people they hated, and in the process, managed to disappear with no consequences at all. They left debts, and dozens of families in ruins.

They left a chair pushed out, and knew that we would assume the worst.

We prosecuted based on that assumption, and received a conviction. And I cleaned up the mess so thoroughly that we have to use photographs and cut pieces of rug, miraculously saved. We can't revisit the scene with Luminol, trying to see what had happened before, because I had smeared it, trying to make the home safe, trying to make it—and us—forget.

We'll never know for certain what happened in that house. Just like we'll never know why another neighbor down the street finished his pie last Thanksgiving and then took his own life.

Just like I'll never know how long my mother lay on the floor of her kitchen, conscious and hoping someone would find her.

We can clean the mess, but the uncertainties remain.

There are Christmas lights around the Moorhead House this year, but there will be no party. It's not in the budget. Once the appeals are over, once the trials have ended, the house will become a museum, just like Louise dreamed.

But people aren't going to go inside to look at one of the city's first houses, thinking about old Josiah Moorhead and the power he had because he had the foresight to build ferries that crossed the river. People will go into his house to see if they can find that one piece of evidence, that one spot of blood, that one thing I might have missed in my thorough cleaning, hoping to see if they can solve the case that nearly cost a group of rowdy and unconventional young people their lives.

I won't go back. I'm not going into any damaged houses any more. I'm strictly management now—assigning teams, paying bills. I can't look at interiors filled with the leftovers of other people's lives, and worry that something important has been missed.

I don't want that responsibility.

My imagination is too strong, my memories too fresh.

I don't need any more ghosts.

I have enough already.

Nutball Season

*I*N MY BUSINESS, NUTBALL SEASON starts on Halloween, and goes to about Christmas. Oh, you get your occasional Friday-the-thirteenth run on the precinct, and you gotta pray you get every full moon off, but the real serious wackos don't seem to surface until about the last week in October, and they don't disappear until New Year's Day. What they do the rest of the year, I haven't the slightest. But up until then, they're harassing me and mine, or folks just like us all over the country.

Every year, I got my favorite nut story. But last year's I don't talk about much. Because I ain't sure exactly who the nut is, me or the geezer what started it all.

You see, he walked into the stationhouse a shade before midnight on December twenty-third, wearing a red Santa suit, and looking pasty and tired, that kinda tired we all get when we pull too many shifts in a row. The house was empty that night. The desk sarge was handling some crisis, the dispatch was doing his nails, for godssake, and most everyone else was either at their own homes or doing their beats.

Me, I was at my desk. I'd stopped in the precinct after a collar to finish up some paperwork before going home to macaroni, cheese and tuna, my specialty. Not that I minded. It was better than Cindy Lou's meatloaf surprise, which I missed even less than I missed her. So I wasn't really in a hurry to leave—even though soaking up the camaraderie of the stationhouse at that time of night was kinda like trying to sleep in a rooms-by-the-hour motel.

The old guy came in as I was typing the last part of my report. He sat down in the metal chair before my desk, leaned over the files like he owned the place and said, "Excuse me."

I held up my hand, signaling he should wait until I was finished, hoping someone else would come into the barren house and the old guy would trot off to them. No luck.

"Excuse me," he said again. "Where do I go to file a complaint?"

I knew I wasn't gonna get rid of him as easy as I wanted so I said, "A complaint about what?"

"Mrs. Billings. She plans to shoot me if I land on her roof tomorrow night."

Now to understand that sentence, you had to know that the next night was Christmas Eve. And since it was Christmas Eve, and he was an elderly guy with a long white beard dressed all in red, it was pretty clear who he was gonna impersonate.

At least, that was how I thought of it at that moment. But I wasn't being quick on the uptake. I didn't think about the implications of asking this guy a question. Which I did.

"Does this Mrs. Billings have a child?"

"Well, of course," the old guy said in his precise way, and I realized then and there that I should have kept my mouth shut because I was buying into his fantasy.

Of course, my mouth hadn't stayed shut, and now I was in deep, and I tried to fix it, I really did. I told him, you know, that maybe he could wait a day or stay off the roof or just plain get outta town.

He looked at me like it was sixth grade again and he was Sister Mary Catherine trying to explain Algebra.

"You simply do not understand," he said. "I cannot stay out of town. I must come, and I must arrive on that night. I cannot change that. Too many children will be disappointed."

"Listen, bub," I said. "I know it's Christmas and all, but you know, kids really can't tell time. They won't notice if Santa arrives on Christmas Eve or the day after."

"They'll notice," he said in that precise way of his. It was his manner of speaking that really got me to look at him. He didn't sound like he was from around here.

I know, I know, I don't exactly sound Upstate either, but you can tell I do belong in New York. This guy sounded kinda English, but kinda like Katherine Hepburn too. You know. Cultured.

And the voice didn't quite suit him either. I mean how do you expect a guy dressed like Santa to sound? Me, I'd think all deep voiced and jolly. But no one'd think jolly about this guy. They wouldn't even think fat. This guy was big, but he was all muscle. His eyes weren't twinkling. They were that hard steel gray that some beat cops get after too many long days. And his beard wasn't snowy white. It was a yellowish silver, the yellow probably being tobacco stains from the pipe clenched tightly in his thin mouth.

"Take it from me," I said to him, "when I was a kid, there was this guy next door who worked for PhilcoFord. This was in the days when companies really cared about their workers, you know? And his guy's kid, he was my age. The company Santa drops by every year, not just to this guy's house, but to ours too, and he always came on a Sunday, but I don't really notice, you know—"

"Not until thirteen year-old Michael Trent pointed it out to you. I know," the geezer said. "He got coal in his stocking that year."

The hair on the back of my neck stood out. The moment was a bit too *Miracle on 34th Street* for me. Now, there coulda been a thousand explanations for him knowing that—I mean I told that story a hundred times—but how he knew he'd get me that night, I couldn't figure.

I decided to ignore the geezer's last comment.

"Anyway," I said. "The point is—"

"That the children don't notice, but they do. They have an internal sense of what's right and what's not, particularly when it comes to Christmas. And that's at the heart of my dilemma."

"How's that?" I ask.

"She has a child. A boy of three. He's a good boy, too, and doesn't ask for much. Her neighbors' children have all grown, and they visit their grandchildren on the holidays, so her son is the only child on the block. Logic dictates that I skip the house, but I simply cannot. In the centuries that I have been doing this work—"

Those hairs rose again. I was gonna have to get them trimmed.

"—I haven't skipped a single child. At least, not a single child who met the criteria."

I didn't want to ask about criteria. I didn't want to know the details. I was sure the old guy would give them to me.

"Mr.—"

"Kringle."

"Yeah, right. Listen, we can visit the lady, ask her to stop threatening you, but without proof or an incident there ain't much we could do. Now you can get yourself a lawyer, and have some judge order her to stay away from you, but even that won't do no good when you go visit her house, don't you see? Maybe there's some other way you can get the presents to the kid."

He stared at me for a moment, and I got the sense, even though he was too polite to say it, that I just didn't get it.

"I have proof," he said softly.

"You do?" For all his complaints against this woman, he never once said nothing about proof. "Well lessee it."

He gave me photocopies—dozens of them—all letters, all from different children, all return addresses right here in our little burg. As he passed the copies to me, he stuck his finger on the top letter and hit it with such force that the sound echoed through the empty precinct.

"Right—" tap "—there."

I glanced at the top letter. It was from a nine-year-old girl. It said that she heard Mrs. Prudence Billings say she'd shoot Santa if he landed on her roof. The little girl, she was writing to warn Santa, and to tell him it was okay if he skipped her this year because she'd rather he'd be safe.

The kid was probably trying to guarantee free presents for life.

Then I thumbed through the letters. They were all versions of the same thing: the kids had heard this Prudence Billings say she'd shoot Santa.

What a great woman. Jeez. What was she doing telling children them things?

"You need a lawyer, Mister," I said, handing the letters back to him.

"But that doesn't solve my dilemma," he said. "I need to go to her house."

"Like I said, get someone else to deliver," and I leaned back in my chair thinking about her poor kid. Imagine having a mom who didn't let you believe in Santa, who didn't let you have that one night when you thought anything was possible, when you actually believed some fat bastard who had flying reindeer could squeeze himself into a space barely wide enough for a broom and give you your heart's desire?

"I can't get someone else to deliver," the geezer said, sounding kinda forlorn. "This isn't a task that can be handed from person to person."

I was feeling a bit bad now. I mean, everyone's entitled to their own delusions if they didn't hurt nobody. But the guy wanted to waste police time on something that wasn't ever gonna happen, and I had to let him know that we didn't send squads chasing after every elf in the bushes, metaphorically speaking.

But then on the other hand, they teach you at the academy to listen to these nuts on the offsides that even nuts sometimes know something what might be true.

So I got to thinking I had this guy figured out, so I leaned forward and I said, "Pop, I know it's tough when families don't get along, and it ain't fair your daughter keeping you away from your grandson, but you know, the kid ain't gonna hold it against you if you get a friend to bring him his toys this year. The kid is gonna be a might upset if his mom takes out the deer rifle and pops you one. I mean if those're your options, you gotta know which one I recommend."

He got up and his voice went all deep, just like I was thinking it shoulda been, except it still wasn't jolly, and he said, "I *hate* going to the established authorities. They never believe me. Why can't you people have an open mind for once?"

The dispatch, he looked up from his nails, and the desk sarge who had come back in from wherever the hell he'd been looked at the old guy throw a fit right in front of me, a very cultured fit, but a fit all the same, and I knew what the sarge was thinking, he was thinking there goes Mantino again, pissing off some citizen.

I'd already heard the lecture about my melancholy state, about the way I should maybe get some help now that Cindy Lou was gone, only the lecture probably wouldn't go that way. It probably would be a bit harsher since Cindy Lou'd been gone nearly six months and my mood hadn't improved much. It was that empty house, you know, the starter, with two bedrooms the size of a closet, and the one empty as a grave, what was supposed to be for the first little Mantino way back when me and Cindy Lou actually liked each other. I'd been spending those last six months thinking, not about Cindy Lou because me and her we weren't right, but about family and how some people want one and never get it and how some people get one and never want it.

All this went through my brain in like a split second, while the geezer's using his elegant voice to broadcast to the whole house how I failed him. So I got up, and I said, not so loud that the sarge could hear, but loud enough to shut up the geezer, "If you got the magic that can make reindeer fly, how come you can't land on a roof without some wacko with a shotgun seeing you?"

The geezer sighed and got back in his chair. The desk sarge looked down, the dispatch went back to his nails, and all was right with the world.

Momentarily.

"The magic works like this," the geezer said. "Anyone who believes in me can see me."

I said, "Look, from what I can see in them letters, she don't believe in you."

"You haven't read closely enough," the old man said. "She believes strongly enough to see me as a threat to the entire civilized world. Unfortunately, she is probably the person who believes in me the most of all the adults in all the world."

He had a point. He had a delusion, she had a delusion, and it was shared and there was a gun mentioned, and I probably shoulda been taking this whole thing a lot more seriously than I had been.

"Okay," I said. "Whatta you want me to do?"

"I want you to go see her," he said, "and make her promise not to shoot me tomorrow night."

"You think that much hate is going to keep a promise?" I ask.

"She's a fanatic, isn't she?" he said. "She should keep a holy vow."

Right. Like I could extract a holy vow from a woman who hated Santa Claus. But it wasn't the hardest thing I'd ever had to do on this job.

So like an idiot, I agreed.

***

CHRISTMAS EVE, MY SHIFT STARTED AT NOON, and since I didn't have a family, I was thinking maybe I'd work late, and then pick up some hours Christmas Day. I wasn't lying to myself that one day was like another; I knew Christmas was special. I just figured if I worked through it, I wouldn't notice.

When I was a kid, the festivities started with the whole advent season. The second the decorations went up in church, they'd go up at home. My mom did the advent calendars and the whole nine yards, and it made December something else. I'd felt the lack ever since I moved from home—it wasn't the same after I'd left, and it got worse after she died—but it was never so bad as on Christmas and Christmas Eve.

I probably shoulda gone to midnight mass. I had it in my head I'd do it when I got off work, but I wasn't sure I wanted to see all them folks and their families in the red velvet and the fake fur coats, and me coming in in my uniform. I didn't figure it'd look right, you know?

And that's what I was trying not to think about as I drove up to this Prudence Billings' house. She lived in one of them ritzy areas of town—you know, those colonial houses with the columns and the eight miles of lawn before you even get to the front door. Santa had not just his choice of roofs, but he had his choice of chimneys here.

I didn't like her even worse than I didn't like her before, and that was before I got outta the squad.

I walked up that long sidewalk alone, noting that whoever shoveled didn't do a fine job as there was still a thin layer of ice that cracked beneath my boots. Someone had salted the steps, and the salt had melted through the ice, but no one'd bothered to kick the ice away, which I did, just as a courtesy.

Then I rang the bell.

The door opened and there was this kid wearing a pair of red shorts and a Santa hat, and grinning like there was no tomorrow. In that face, I saw every devil that ever walked and I knew that the geezer lied.

This kid wasn't good, he was hell on wheels, and I was just about to give him flight.

I caught him with one arm as he was about to sail into the snowy depths of the yard.

"Hey, kiddo," I said. "You ain't dressed for winter."

"Don't care," he said, struggling against me.

I wrapped my arm around him, lifted him off the ground and stepped inside with him. The hallway was one of them all wood jobbies with a staircase going up the side. The banister was covered in pine boughs, and there were ornaments hanging every which way.

"Miles?" a woman's voice shouted from above.

"He's down here," I said, hoping I didn't give her too much of a start. "I caught him going out the door."

I heard someone running across the floor upstairs, and then this girl peeked around the banister. Only it took me a half second to realize that wasn't no girl. That was a woman about my age who managed not only to keep her figure, but to keep lines off her face as well. Only her eyes told me she'd seen more of the world than any twenty-year-old ever could.

"And you are?" she asked, like someone in a uniform stood in her entry every day of the week.

"Name's Mantino, ma'am," I said with as much dignity as a man could muster when a three-year-old was squirming over his left arm, and kicking him perilously close to his private parts. "I'm with the police."

"I would hope so," she said. "Would you mind closing the door? It's got to be at least 20 degrees out there."

"Eighteen, ma'am," I said mostly because she had me a bit flustered. I didn't expect a person named Prudence Billings to look like this, kinda like a ballet dancer only without the ugly feet.

"Miles," she said, "where did you get that hat?"

The kid froze like he'd been dipped in ice, and truth be told, I kinda did too. I only heard one other woman on earth use that tone, and it was my mother back when I knew she'd caught me at something but good. My backside was twitching, and I would wager Miles's was too.

Still, he lifted his head over my bicep and grinned that Ain't-I-Cute? grin. "Got it at school," he said.

"Well, take it off," she said. "You know we don't allow that rubbish in here."

"Ma—"

"Miles."

He looked up at me and whispered, "Sorry but I gotta go now," and squirmed his way outta my arm. Then he tossed the hat at me like I gave it to him, and took off like a bat outta hell in the opposite direction. From that way, I smelled Christmas cookies, so I was wagering he was off to the kitchen to torment some poor housekeeper.

The lady sighed and came down the stairs. She was barefoot like I said, and her toenails were painted red and green and decorated with sprinkles that accent the colors. When she stopped on the landing, I noticed she wasn't quite as tall as I was. I figured when she was standing flat-foot on the floor she wasn't even gonna come up to my shoulders.

"What can I do for you, officer?"

I was twisting the red hat around in my hands like it was mine. She held out her hand for it, and I gave it to her. Her fingernails were long and painted just the same way. She didn't wear any rings.

"Prudence Billings?"

"Yes," she said.

I glanced at the hallway, lowered my voice, and then said, "I got some geezer come to the stationhouse last night saying you've been threatening Santa Claus."

She laughed. The sound was like a series of bells ringing on a starry night. "I have been."

I nearly took off my hat and started twisting it in my hands. "You said if he landed on your roof, you'd take a shotgun after him?"

"I said it to anyone who'd listen, Officer."

"Did you mean it?"

She looked at me, and I got the sense that this woman didn't do nothing she didn't mean. "Why do you ask?"

"Like I said, we gotta complaint—"

"Yes, I know. But not many folks would follow up on it. After all, my threat is only good if some man dressed in a red suit has his flying reindeer land a sleigh on my roof. In fact, I won't really do anything unless he slides down my chimney. I don't plan to sit on the lawn with the gun in my lap."

"Good thing," I said, "since it ain't something the neighbors would appreciate."

She laughed even though I was serious. So I got just a tad more serious.

"You gotta license for that shotgun?"

Her smile didn't just fade, it vanished like it never was, and I knew I had a lady who knew nothing about guns at all. A lady, a gun, and a kid. I didn't like how this was shaping up.

"'Fraid you gotta give it to me." I figured I'd keep it for the next few days, and the geezer wouldn't got nothing to worry about. By then maybe she'd rethink the whole gun-owning business. And if she didn't I'd give her a stern lecture when I got back on gun responsibility.

She stood on the landing, and said, "If you take the gun, will you protect me?"

"Seems to me that's a husband's job, ma'am," I said.

She looked up at me, and anger flared in her pretty eyes. I kinda liked the spark.

"Well, seeing as I don't have a husband, I'm relying on either myself or the police for protection."

"Protection from what, ma'am?"

"Santa Claus."

I sighed. I couldn't help it. "You know, ma'am, seems to me there's a lot more to worry about in this world than a man in a red suit who lands on your roof."

"You don't see it my way."

"No, ma'am. I always thought Santa was one of those guys who brought a little joy in the world, if you know what

I mean, ma'am." I was treading lightly here because while this broad was one of the most beautiful creatures I'd ever seen, she was probably some religious nut, and I wasn't in the mood to argue the religious implications of jolly ole St. Nick.

"He doesn't always bring joy," she said.

"No, he don't. Sometimes he misses kids. But the fire department and us, we do what we can to make sure them kids get something."

"To keep up the myth." Her voice was rising. I knew then I'd made some kinda mistake.

"Well, you know, it's kinda nice to have something to believe in." Then I winced, thinking she'd launch into the Jesus lecture, you know, the putting Christ back into Christmas thingie.

"No, it's not," she said, and I looked at her. I mean really looked at her.

This lady was scared.

So I said, "Tell me why you're doing this. It ain't natural to have something against Santa Claus."

"I'm trying to protect my son."

She *was* a loony. I sorta let the sigh out this time. "Lady, Santa leaves presents. I ain't never once heard a story where he traded 'em for the kids."

"That's not it," she said. "You saw him." And at first, I'm thinking she meant Santa Claus. Then I realize she meant the kid.

"Yeah," I said. "He's a pistol."

"Exactly." She came the rest of the way down the stairs and I was right. She didn't come up to my shoulders. But she smelled like roses, all delicate and fragile. "Miles is just like my brother."

"Is that a good thing, ma'am?"

"Not in this case. You're new to town, aren't you, officer?"

"Been here more'n two years, ma'am."

She shook her head. "When he was little, my brother fell off that roof and died. Broke his neck, which was probably for the best or so they tell me, since we didn't find him until Christmas morning. By then he was frozen stiff."

I didn't like how this was going. "I'm sorry to hear it, ma'am."

"He was seven. He was up there to watch Santa land." She swallowed. "My son is just like him. I don't want him to get wrapped up in the Santa myth. I'm afraid he'll do the same thing, and then I'll lose him too."

Her voice broke a little, and I put a hand on her shoulder. She didn't seem to mind.

"Look, ma'am," I said, feeling for her, knowing that we all go a little crazy over the things that hurt us most. "Your son ain't your brother—"

"I know," she said, "but I worry. And I think the best thing is to let him know that Santa isn't real, so then he'll avoid the whole thing. And he would be able to if the town didn't buy into this. I tried to prevent them from doing so, but it didn't work. Everyone still talks about Santa, and you've seen what it does to my son. He's got his Santa hat, and he's ready to show me that I'm wrong."

"Well, I think you are, ma'am," I said. "Santa ain't about materialism, not really, if you think about it. He's kinda a cherished cultural whatchamacallit—"

"Icon," she said.

"Yeah, whatever," I said. "He's one of them. Not because he brings us stuff, but because we think he does." That didn't come out the way I wanted it to so I took a deep breath and started over. "What I'm trying to say is this guy is okay to believe in because he's like pure good, you know. How many other examples do we got of someone who spends his whole year making stuff for others, then gives it all away in one night—to everyone, no one left out?"

"That's not how it works."

"Ain't it?" I said. "I been on various police forces for the last twenty years, and in all that time, I never seen a kid get missed by Santa, even if the Santa was a Toys for Tots program."

"If Santa was real," she said, "my brother wouldn't be dead."

"Ah, lady." I wanted to crouch down, face her at eye level and talk to her like a kid, because that's what she was sounding like. Some little teeny kid. "How old was you when all this came down?"

"Three," she whispered.

You didn't have to be no rocket scientist to figure out who she was protecting here, and it wasn't that underage demon in the red pants munchin' cookies in the kitchen.

"Look," I said, "You give me your shotgun, and I'll come back here when I'm off duty. I'll make sure Miles stays in his room, and Santa stays outside."

She raised her head. Her eyes were wide, and I thought I'd never seen anything so pretty in my whole life.

"You'd do that?" she asked. "Why?"

"Let's just say I think every kid needs a little guaranteed joy once a year, and three's too young to have it snatched away from you. Besides," I smiled at her. "I met your kid. He seems to me to be the type who'd go to the roof to prove to you that Santa *does* exist."

"I've been worried about that," she said. "I just hoped if I talked about it enough, the whole town would forget about this nonsense."

"It ain't nonsense, and no one'll forget," I said. "We all remember what it's like to be a kid and having that hope on Christmas Eve. We ain't gonna give it up, and we ain't gonna deny our kids the same thing."

"Do you have kids, officer?" she asked.

"I ain't found the right woman to have them with," I said.

She put a small hand on the side of my face. "Some woman doesn't know what she's missing," she said. Then she went upstairs, and brought me the gun.

***

I WORKED MY REGULAR SHIFT, got off around eight, and flew outta the stationhouse. The dispatch, he made some crack about me having a date, and the whole group laughed like it wasn't possible, but I didn't say nothing. I just drove to the Billings place, hoping I wasn't too early. As it was, they was waiting for me.

Prudence Billings opened the door when I pulled up out front and motioned me inside. The pistol was wearing feet pajamas and his Santa cap, and holding a plate of cookies. I was thinking this kid wasn't gonna sleep for two weeks, judging by the brightness in his eyes.

"Miz Billings?" I'd changed into jeans and my heavy winter coat, figuring I was spending the night outside, waiting for the jingle of tiny sleigh bells.

"Priddy," she said.

"Ah, beg pardon?"

"Call me Priddy," she said. "Everyone does." Then she grinned. "It's better than Prude."

"Much," I said, thinking it seemed more accurate too. The house was looking nice. There was a tree in the living room, and white lights on the evergreen boughs on the stairs. The place was fairly bursting to be festive, and I figured it wouldn't take a lot of work to get Priddy Billings to start celebrating in a way that'd satisfy the kid.

"I got cookies for you, Mister," the pistol said.

"Thanks," I said, and took one. It was a sugar cookie with a bit too much frosting, but it had a sweet lemony taste like the ones my mom used to make. The taste of Christmas, sure as I breathed.

"It's officer," Priddy was saying to the kid. "Officer Mantino."

"Actually," I said, "it's Nick."

She grinned. "How appropriate," she said.

I guess it was. I never thought of it that way. "Well," I said, "what's the plan?"

"The plan is to get Miles to bed, and then I'll hold down the inside while you guard the outside."

"Seems fair," I said. "You ready to sleep, sport?"

"I'm not gonna sleep," he said. "I'm gonna show Mom that Santa's coming."

Priddy closed her pretty eyes.

"Well," I said, crouching down to be at his level. "You ain't gonna do that by staying awake."

"Why not?" the kid asked.

"You don't know?" I said. "Santa don't come to houses where kids are awake."

I thought Priddy's mouth was gonna fall off her face. I guess she hadn't thought of that one. It was a simple solution to her problem. Keep the kid awake all night and Santa wouldn't show up. Too late now. I'd spilled the beans.

"That true?" the kid asked.

"Scouts honor," I said, holding up my hand.

"You was a scout?" he asked.

"Eagle," I said, not lying.

"Wow," he said. "You know, I wanna be a scout."

"*Miles*," Priddy said in that voice again.

"Ah, Mom," he said, but started up the stairs anyway. Halfway up, he stopped. "You wanna read to me, Mister?"

"Officer Mantino has done enough." Priddy marched past me and went with the kid. "He'll be guarding the house tonight, so you say thank you."

"Thank you," the kid said. "Merry Christmas."

That last was a little forlorn, so I grinned at him. "Merry Christmas, sport."

Then he trudged the rest of the way up the stairs. She followed. I wandered into the living room, wondering if she really wanted me to snoop that far into their lives. The tree was big and green and smelled like pine heaven. Under it were more presents than I'd received since I'd grown up, all in that shiny wrapping paper that reflected the lights.

The lady wasn't loony. She was just fighting something she shoulda dealt with long ago. She'd mixed up believing in Santa with the death of her brother, and then with the growing up of her kid. I was really glad now I got the shotgun outta the house. I wasn't looking forward to a night in the snow, but I figured it was a small price to pay for what I hoped was a chance to take Priddy Billings to dinner—when the holidays was over and she turned back into a normal person again.

It took her a while, but she finally came down the stairs. I was back in the hallway by then. She put a finger to her lips and led me into the kitchen. In there, I saw the remains of a Christmas ham. She handed me a bag filled with sandwiches and a thermos of coffee.

"Sorry to send you out on a night like this."

I shrugged. It wasn't a bad night. Just cold. "I volunteered."

"You're a nice man," she said.

"I got my moments."

"You think I'm crazy, don't you?"

That's one of them trick questions. If I said yes, I doomed this friendship for life. If I said no, I'd be lying. "I think you got issues," I said.

"You're polite too," she said.

I set the bag and the thermos on the table, then pulled my gloves outta my pocket and put my wool cap over my ears. "I'd better get out there."

"You think he'll come this early?"

"Priddy." I liked the way the name sounded when I said it. "I don't think he'll come at all, but I think we should be vigilant now, just in case."

"Good point," she said, and went back upstairs. She stopped at the kitchen door. "Thank you, Nick."

"You're welcome," I said, and let myself out the back.

***

I WASN'T GONNA HIDE. I thought the worst thing I could do was wedge myself behind some bush and freeze to death, making Priddy relive her Christmas horror, and giving the kid a bad fright too. I had this all figured. In my car were a few things that a sales clerk assured me a three-year-old boy would like. I was gonna give 'em to Priddy around dawn, before the kid was up. I figured it was up to her to say whether the stuff came from me, a stranger, or Santa, a made-up stranger.

Maybe by then, she'd be willing to acknowledge Santa. If we made it through the night without him, that is. And I figured we would. First, you know, adult common sense said there was no such thing as Santa. But if there was, no self-respecting Santa would show up when people were looking for him. But I did figure there was a chance the geezer would come, and I kinda wanted to head him off at the pass. Maybe sometime in the next year, him and Priddy would resolve whatever differences they had. Maybe I'd still be around to help 'em do it.

So that's what I was thinking. I trudged around the yard, wearing a hole in the snow that probably wasn't doing the lawn any good. I watched the neighbors lights go out one by one, and I sucked down too much coffee and had to wait until one whole side of the neighborhood was dark before getting rid of some of it.

I think it was long about one a.m. when I got the bright idea to get the ice off Priddy's sidewalk. It was too late to use a shovel—that scrape-scrape-scrape would wake up the dead—so I decided to use my boot.

I was working my way from the porch to the road when I saw something move on the roof. I let out a four-banger blue alarm cuss that woulda sent me packing if Priddy heard it, and stepped back for a better look.

Damned if the geezer wasn't there, in his red suit and red hat, and looking jolly. Behind him was reindeer—at least some kinda deer—hooked onto a sleigh that was made of dark wood with red trim. It had curled runners, and the back end was piled high with toy sacks.

The geezer held up his mittened hand and waved at me. Then he hoisted himself onto the chimney, and I started cussing again. I mean, what was I gonna do to stop him, pelt him with snowballs? By the time I got to the back door, the geezer'd disappeared through the chimney and I was praying to every god I could think of that Priddy hadn't hid another weapon where I couldn't see it.

I slid through the back door, and tracked sludge on the linoleum. I slammed open the swinging doors, hurried through the decorated hallway, and stopped in the living room.

There he was, crouched beside the tree, laying train tracks—bright yellow and blue PlaySkool® train tracks with a big fat engine just perfect for a three-year-old. He set a kid-sized basketball hoop on the antique chair beside the fireplace, and put a small basketball beneath it. Then he turned around and pointed at me.

"I expect you to make sure he uses this," the geezer said in that prim tone of his.

"Me?" I said, looking behind me, thinking maybe Priddy was there. But she wasn't. I could hear her light step on the floor above. "Hey, you didn't tell me the whole story."

"But I do want to thank you," the geezer said. "I didn't see a shotgun."

"I got the shotgun," I said. "But she has a legitimate gripe. Her brother died on Christmas Eve. He fell off the roof. You got magic. How come you didn't do nothing?"

The jolly left the geezer's face. Suddenly it was like he was eighty years older than he'd been before.

"Magic has limitations," he said. "Mine is limited to this kind of joyfulness. Do you know how many little children ask me to get their mommies and daddies back together or to put an end to war? I can't. I don't have the power."

"You got the power to grab some kid who's sliding off a roof," I said, and there was a bit of force behind my words. You know, if this guy was who he said he was—and he had to be, didn't he?, I seen the deer—then I'd been idolizing him for some time. I coulda caught a kid with one hand, and pulled him to safety. This geezer coulda too.

"No, I don't," he said. "And you know why."

"The hell I do," I said.

He squinted at me.

"Because," he said, "I don't come to houses where people are awake."

"I'm awake."

"Yes, I know," he said. "But I asked you for help. It's a slightly different circumstance. And I wouldn't be here if Miles weren't sleeping. Soundly."

"So you didn't come at all that night, the night the kid died?"

"Ask Miss Billings," the geezer said, looking over my shoulder.

I turned. She was behind me, looking small. Her eyes were bright with unspent tears. They reflected the tree lights.

"You didn't come, did you?" she said in that little kid voice. "There were no special presents under the tree. I remember now. I hadn't thought of that. It hadn't seemed like Christmas that day. You didn't come because I was awake. I was waiting for my brother to come back to bed. Oh, God," she said, and her voice broke. "I killed him."

"No," I said.

"No," the geezer said at the same time. Only he went on. "It was one of those things that magic doesn't have a solution to. I'm so very sorry."

We were silent for what seemed like forever, waiting to see what Priddy would do. Finally, she blinked and one of the tears fell. Then she looked at the tree.

"Are those for Miles?" she asked.

"Yes," the geezer said.

"Wait," she said, and disappeared around the corner. I was hoping that she didn't go to do something stupid, but I didn't stop her. It was between her and the geezer now.

"You coulda told me," I said.

"You had to discover it for yourself," the geezer said.

"Why?" I ask.

He smiled. "Because I can't do anything without making a gift out of it."

"A gift?" I say.

He nodded, and then Priddy came back into the room. She was carrying that plate of cookies that Miles had out for me, and a glass of milk.

"We need to follow the tradition," she said.

The geezer took one of the cookies, and ate it. He grabbed the rest of the cookies and shoved them in his pocket—"for the reindeer," he said around the food—all except one, a Santa whose red suit was a bit too pink. He bit the head off it, and left it and a bunch of crumbs on the plate. "A tradition," he said and swallowed. He took the milk from Priddy, drank it all, and handed her the glass back. His mustache was dripping.

He looked at Priddy. "I'm glad this is finally settled."

"Between us it's settled," she said. "But it'll never be all right."

That sad look was back on his face. "My dear, things like this are never all right. But we do learn how to go on living, despite the pain."

"I guess we do," she said.

Then he smiled at her. "There is a gift for you here, too," he said. "If you only see it."

She looked at the tree. I was watching him. He put a finger alongside his nose, gave me a nod—and just like in the damn poem—up the chimney he rose.

Priddy looked back at me.

"He's gone," she said.

"Yep," I said. Then I cleared my throat. "I guess you won't be needing me no more."

She put a hand on my arm. "It was kind of you to give up your family time to help us."

I shrugged. "Ain't got family no more, ma'am. So it was no bother at all."

She looked at me, like she was seeing me for the first time. "Then I insist you stay. We have a guest room, and a Christmas turkey that's too big for Miles and me."

"I couldn't," I said. "It's a family day."

"It's no bother," she said. "Really. You helped us. I'd like to repay you." Then I grinned. She meant it. She really did. "I got stuff for Miles in the car."

"You were going to be Santa," she said.

"I think it's important," I said.

She glanced at the chimney.

"I guess it's important," she said, "even when we don't admit it."

"Especially then," I said.

***

Now I wouldn'ta told you all this except in the context that we been discussing nutcases. You see, the next morning, over Priddy's protests, I went out on that roof, and there weren't no sleigh marks or footprints or hoof prints. There wasn't no soot on Priddy's polished floor neither, and later I found a receipt for one basketball hoop, child-sized, by the cookie jar in the pantry.

I woulda thought Priddy was humbugging us all with them threats while celebrating like everyone else did if I hadn't come down with a humdinger of a cold from standing outside for too long on an icy December night. Priddy brought me her housekeeper's famous chicken soup and she took care of me during that awful week.

We've become something of a thing, you know, me and Priddy, and the guys at the stationhouse think it's funny; some woman from old money hooking up with a guy like me. But they don't know that we have lots to share, her and me. I'm the one who believes in stuff; she's the one who needs to. She's the one with the family; I'm the one who needs one. Stuff like that.

We're gonna make it official next Christmas season, but we're getting a new house. Something between my starter and her colonial, something that's just ours. It'll have a roof, but nothing too high, so if the kid gets adventurous—and he won't, not while I'm around—he won't get killed if he slips off.

I just keep thinking about the geezer, you know? I keep thinking maybe we should invite him to the wedding. After all, he's the one what brought us together. And I wonder if we send a wedding invite to that North Pole address the kids use, if he'll get it, and if he gets it, will he show?

Then I think about what I'm worrying about, and I check to see if it's a full moon or something. You know. Nutball season.

Because there's a part of me that's still embarrassed I believe in the old guy, even though I do. Since he was right. He gave all three of us a gift that night.

He gave the kid Christmas and he gave me and Priddy each other.

And that's enough to make anyone believe in Santa—even nutballs. Like me.

Loop

*A*MELIA COULD NOT BELIEVE SHE was actually sitting there. The log was cold and damp beneath her jeans. The trees above dripped water. Out in the mist, an owl called, followed by the faint echo of a dog barking. Laughter from the porch made her cringe.

Above the ground fog, the sky was clear. Stars twinkled and a tiny satellite made its consistent way around the heavens. Her cheeks tingled with chill.

She could still feel the controls, clutched in her left palm. The sharp plastic edges bit into her skin.

Somehow she hadn't imagined it would be like this. Somehow she had thought the device would send her into the middle of an extended memory: *she* would be sitting on the porch, Tyler's hand warm on her knee, Jeanne and Paul beside them, the smell of eggnog in the air. She had wanted to relive it all, not observe it from the side.

"More eggnog anyone?" Tyler's voice had a deep richness. It warmed her. She longed to crawl onto the porch, knock her old self out of the way, and sit beside him again.

She had tried that when she first arrived. Her hands went through them all—and they hadn't noticed. She felt like Emily in *Our Town*: trapped in the best memory of her life, and no one saw her.

"Me," her own voice replied. It sounded higher, more confident than it did from the inside.

"Yeah, and a little more rum," Paul said.

"None for me." Jeannie's southern accent had an air of falseness. Amelia didn't remember her well. Paul had broken up with Jeanne after dating her for only a year.

A long time ago.

It had all been a long time ago.

Amelia got up off the log, brushed the water off her jeans (—how could she feel that and not her friends on the porch?—), and let herself in the back door. The kitchen was as she remembered it: done in browns and tans, filled with too many dishes, too many books and too many papers. The room smelled like turkey and pumpkin pies cooled on the counter. A calico cat—Nerdboy! She hadn't thought of Nerdboy in years—slept on an overstuffed kitchen chair.

Tyler stood over a large punchbowl filled with egg-nog batter. With his right hand, he poured a steaming bowl of hot rum into the mixture. His dark hair curled over his collar, and his broad shoulders strained at his denim workshirt.

She had forgotten how slim he was, how graceful his

movements. As she walked toward him, Nerdboy looked up. His tail thumped against the chair, and his ears went back. He growled.

Tyler half-turned. "What is it, Nerdie?"

She froze there, waiting for him to see her. Nerdboy growled again.

"There's nothing there, kiddo," Tyler said, and returned to the eggnog. In the living room, the opening strains of the Elvis Presley version of "Blue Christmas" blared before someone turned the stereo down.

"Hey, you hiding in there or what?" Paul yelled.

"Coming!" Tyler ladled eggnog into three glass cups, looped his fingers through the handles, and carried them into the living room. Amelia followed. A fifteen foot Douglas fir dwarfed the room, decorated only in colored lights and clear glass balls. Elvis crooned in the background, and brightly wrapped packages huddled under the tree. Her younger self patted the couch for Tyler. He handed Paul a cup before sitting down.

Her younger self looked up and the smile froze on her face. She grabbed Tyler's wrist, nearly spilling some eggnog on his shirt. "Tyler, look. There she is again. That woman."

Tyler set his cup on the coffee table before looking up. Amelia didn't move. She wanted them to see her. She wanted *him* to see her. "Hon, it's shadows."

"No," Paul said. "I see someone too." He stepped out of the living room. Amelia walked toward him. If Paul believed, then Tyler would too. Then she could touch him again—

She squeezed the controls tightly, holding her breath as Paul walked into the darkened hallway. The machine squealed, and light shattered around her.

***

She could see nothing for what felt like an eternity. Then the white light faded into red and green spots. The air was warm, warmer than it had been in the house. She didn't move, uncertain of where she was.

The spots cleared and she found herself in the lab. The lab was as empty as it had been when she got there hours—a day?—ago. The forlorn Christmas tree left a pile of needles on the tiled floor. The Happy Holidays banner had come loose from its nails and the middle sagged. Dirty cups sat on the worktables and gift-wrap overflowed from the wastebaskets.

It took a moment before she focused on the figure sitting in the middle of the mess. It was another version of herself—the version she had seen in the mirror that morning—fifty-six, slightly overweight, with deep, sad lines forming around her mouth, and silver hairs overpowering the black ones in her short haircut.

Something was wrong. She shouldn't be able to see herself. Not here. Not in the now. She should be *in* herself, experiencing the moment from the inside.

Perhaps that was a moment from her past. Perhaps that was what she had looked like before she had gone to the memory. Perhaps she hadn't come all the way back.

She looked down at the controls, but they were still hidden by that incredibly bright light. She couldn't feel her left hand.

Tyler would have known what to do. Tyler always test-ran the equipment, while she stayed back and monitored the progress from the Now-station. Only no one was monitoring for her. No one could see if the small red malfunction light was blinking.

It would be so easy, she had said to herself after having too much rum and eggnog alone in that big empty house. *Just a little trip back, set for only ten minutes: routine. No one would argue with routine.*

No one would even notice. No one was scheduled to return to the lab until the day after New Year's, and that was Mark and Christy, the junior team, who would test all the equipment to see if everything was running properly for the week's experiments. Mark and Christy were grad students who had only been on the Project since Tyler died. Even if they saw the malfunction button blinking, they wouldn't know what to do about it.

Not that it mattered. No one had survived in the time stream this long. Tyler had thought it impossible to last more than a day. The government forensic experts who had autopsied him had thought some temporal distortion had killed him. They had warned her to pick the next traveler carefully—someone young with a lot of stamina and no family history of severe medical problems. Having anyone else travel would jeopardize the government funding and the Defense Department approval.

Amelia didn't know how long she had been in the stream. Tyler had never mentioned a white light.

She closed her eyes and reached for her left hand. Her fingers encountered fabric. She followed it until she felt her left wrist bone—with her right hand, as if it were someone else's wrist—then slid her fingers around to the controls. The plastic was cold. She couldn't feel any of the indented keys. She fumbled, reached, and heard an explosion loud as a clap of thunder.

***

THE SUN WARMED HER FACE. Her back was wet. An odd tingling ran up her left side. Her left arm had gone to sleep. She opened her eyes and found herself staring at a sky so blue it looked like it had been painted by a child who loved bright colors.

Water lapped around her, pushing at her clothes, raising her off the ground and then retreating. A hesitant lover, uncertain of his touch. She smiled and reached for Tyler as she had every morning since she was twenty-five.

He was gone.

She sat up, memory returning. Her left arm dragged in the sand, the control fused to her hand as if she too were made of some sort of synthetic. The sand was white, the air humid. The branches on the palm trees swayed with the gentle breeze. To her left the ocean stretched as far as she could see. To her right, the beach ended in a rise that led to a modified Spanish adobe.

Amelia had never been here before.

She stood. Her arm swung heavy and useless beside her. Water dripped off her hair, and down her clothes. Her tennis shoes were soaked. That sensation bothered her most of all. She slipped off one shoe, then the other, picked them up and walked barefoot across the hot sand.

Halfway to the adobe, her feet encountered stone. The stone path led through a hedge of oversized ferns. She walked through it and stood on a rise overlooking a shaded verandah. Small groups of white wicker furniture surrounded a small swimming pool. Two large glass doors were propped open. Thin white curtains blew inside the house, revealing more white furniture and a white carpet. A serving tray bearing a glass filled with brown liquid floated by itself through the double doors. It stopped near one of the furniture groupings.

"…can't." A woman's voice floated up toward Amelia. Amelia walked down the rise beside the pool, looking for the source of the voice.

A young woman sat in one of the wicker lounge chairs, slim legs crossed at the ankles. She wore a sheer white wrap with bikini bottoms underneath. Her feet were bare. Her right hand rested on a glass table, the beverage beside her. The serving unit floated back toward the house.

"I know this isn't the most festive place to spend Christmas. But—" her voice broke "—Grandmama's funeral is tomorrow, and all the relatives will already be here."

Amelia couldn't see the phone at all, but she knew it had to be there. The young woman was speaking into the air. Amelia wondered how the young woman heard the voice on the other end. She walked closer, remaining half-hidden, uncertain if the young woman could see her.

Then she stopped. The young woman had long black hair, a narrow face, and wide dark eyes.

She looked like Tyler.

She looked exactly like Tyler.

Amelia sat on one of the wicker chairs near the pool. Her left hand bumped the edge of the chair, sending a dull ache to her shoulder. The unit squealed and light eased out of its sides. The fingers on her right hand tingled.

A lump rose in her throat. She and Tyler had never had children. On purpose. So what had brought her here, to this woman, near Christmas? It was somewhere beyond Now, somewhere in the future, judging by the devices. Had Tyler had a child he hadn't told her about? He had had so many relationships before they met.

"No, look. I'm sorry," the young woman said. "I can't talk any more." She moved her right hand slightly and sighed. The connection had been severed somehow. Then she sat forward and squinted in Amelia's direction.

"Grandmama?"

The young woman reached for Amelia.

"Grandmama?" she repeated.

The light grew brighter. Amelia reached back. Their fingers met, but did not touch. Instead, the light engulfed her, and she could no longer see.

***

THE GIFTS WERE OPEN. Brightly colored wrapping paper lay in shreds on the floor. Paul and Tyler sat cross-legged on the hardwood floor, playing with matchbox trucks. Jeanne and Amelia's younger self leaned on the back of the couch, arms crossed, and made snide comments about boys always being boys.

Amelia stood next to Paul. His red truck slid across the floor and went through her feet. Her entire left side tingled, and the tingle had grown in her right fingers. She wanted to kneel next to Tyler and ask him what was happening. She wanted him to reassure her that everything was all right.

But everything was not all right. She was wasting away. Tyler had had the same symptoms, spread over a longer period.

She crouched, her left hand scraping the smooth wood floor. Paul started, then slid back, grabbing Tyler's arm as he moved. "There she is," Paul said.

"Where?" Amelia's younger self stepped forward. Jeanne followed.

Tyler looked up. "I don't see anything."

"Jesus," Paul said. "It looks like your mother, Amelia."

"Mother was never in this house," Amelia's younger self said.

Amelia remained still. She met Paul's gaze steadily.

"Where?" Tyler asked.

"Right next to me," Paul said.

Suddenly Tyler saw her. She recognized the light in his eyes. "My God," he said. He got up and walked around her. She stifled the urge to move with him. Then he tried to put his hand on her shoulder. She leaned into the touch, but his hand went right through her.

"My God," he repeated. "This isn't your mother, Amelia. This is you."

Amelia nodded. Tyler jumped back.

"This isn't possible," Amelia's younger self said. "I'm right here. I'm alive."

"And so is she." Tyler crouched in front of Amelia. His cheeks were flushed. "You can hear me, can't you?"

"Yes," she said.

"Yes," he whispered. "But I can't hear you." He tried to touch her again, and frowned as his hand went through her. "It's some kind of distortion field. You're not a ghost at all."

"I'm alive," Amelia said. She had to repeat it twice before Tyler understood.

"It is a distortion field. Time experiments?"

The older Tyler would have yelled at her for giving his younger self that much information, but she didn't know what it would hurt now. He had already seen her.

She nodded.

"My God," he said. "They work."

She shook her head and touched her arm. "Help me," she said. "Please. Help me."

"She's asking for help," Paul said. "Tyler—"

But Paul's voice was fading. The light had returned:

brighter this time. It burned into her left hand, along her side. She cried out in pain—and then the light engulfed her.

***

COLORS FLASHED BEHIND HER CLOSED EYELIDS. She was on a cold, hard floor. Her head ached. She sat up and rubbed her forehead with her good hand before opening her eyes.

The lab again. Her Now-self still huddled over the controls like they were her last link to sanity. She stared at her Now-self for a moment. Had she really looked that lost before stepping into the time stream? She used to pity women who looked like that after they had lost their man. Tyler had been dead six months. She still had the experiments, their house, their friends.

But they all felt so empty without him. An ache grew in her chest.

It's a dream, Tyler had said. *We're living a dream.*

She made herself get up. She swayed a bit, unused to moving without the help of her left arm. She walked around the benches to her Now-Self. Her Now-self was fiddling with the controls. Amelia remembered that moment: she only had time to return to one memory. She had to make it a good one.

Odd that she hadn't picked one with her and Tyler alone.

But she had been thinking Christmas, since it was the loneliness of the holidays that had driven her to the lab in the first place. And the best Christmas had been that first one in the country house, with Paul and Jeanne. She and Paul and Tyler had always compared the others to that one, thinking that nothing could measure up.

But it didn't really seem that special now. Perhaps it had been special because it had been the first.

Her Now-self looked up and gasped. Amelia sat on the bench across from her. Her Now-self reached out just as the air exploded around them.

***

SHE COULDN'T GET AIR. Her mouth was filled with water. Her right arm flailed. She opened her eyes to a blue distorted world. Underwater. She was under water. She had to reach the surface or she would drown.

She kicked up, three good strong kicks that pushed her to the air. She spit the water out of her mouth and took deep, thankful breaths. Water rippled around her. Her presence had disturbed it. She was in a pool. The pool she had seen near the adobe house. She kicked her way to the ladder on the pool's deep end, and grabbed onto the metal railing with her right hand. The tingling had progressed into her wrist. She could barely move the hand at all.

She was running out of time.

She climbed out and sat on the side, breathing heavily. The young woman was asleep in her lounge chair, left arm covering her beautiful face. Amelia knew better than to try and touch her. The people were not real but the places were, as if they were a revolving set for a cosmic play.

Amelia grabbed a towel off the stack and wiped the water from her face. The humid air almost felt cool. She wrapped the towel around her neck, and wandered inside the house.

The main room was white with white furniture: obviously for entertaining. The back rooms had beds in them with clothes scattered about. The young woman did not live alone. A cat slept in the middle of one of the beds, and gave Amelia the evil eye as she passed.

She stopped in the only bedroom that looked as if it hadn't been used recently. The bed was an oversized four-poster like the one she and Tyler had had, with pale pink sheets under a pink and brown patterned spread. But that wasn't what drew her. What drew her were the pictures on the walls.

Some looked familiar: an early date with Tyler at a seafood place; a prize-winning photo of their first lab. But others were dream photos: her in a white wedding gown, Tyler in a black tux smiling down at her; both of them smiling in professional photography fashion at the tiny baby she held in her arms. Then baby pictures and school pictures of a young girl surrounded by family groupings with Tyler aging as he had and the temporal distortion wasting him away. He wore another tux for the young girl's wedding, looking proud and fatherly, and after that, he appeared in no more pictures even though they continued to chronicle the girl, and then her daughter—the young woman Amelia had seen outside.

She sighed and leaned on the bed. Her body was shaking. A life that she hadn't lived, complete with photographs. This had probably been her room until she died.

The shaking turned into a shudder. A life she hadn't lived. A life she could never live, even if she had married Tyler and had a child. She would die in this time stream—in this loop—and no one would know. They would just think she had disappeared.

She stared at the photos, and watched as they vanished in a blur of light.

***

SHE AWOKE TO THE SOUND OF VOICES. Tyler was hunched over her, a frown on his too-young face. "She's back," he said.

Amelia couldn't move either arm. She wanted to sit up, but knew she didn't dare, not in front of this young Tyler, not with the chance of losing her balance.

"What's happening to you?" he asked.

She wished he could hear her. She would tell him and maybe he would find a solution. Still, it wouldn't hurt to try. "I'm trapped," she said. "I'm stuck in a loop."

He understood the part about being trapped. She had to repeat herself three times before he said: "Loop? Like in the movies?"

Not exactly, because she did move forward in each time period. She just kept visiting the same three settings. But she nodded anyway.

"Loop," he said reflectively. The tree lights winked behind him.

"I still think she's a ghost," Paul said, from somewhere behind them. "I don't care about the scar on the chin. She looks like Amelia's mother."

Tyler shook his head just a little. He smiled at her with the love she had missed. He knew her, just as she would have known him. It didn't matter that she had a younger self watching somewhere in the background.

The light was back, eating Tyler, making him disappear. The loops were shorter now. "Tyler," she said, wishing she could reach for him. She didn't want to lose him again—

***

—BUT WHEN SHE CAME TO HERSELF she was back in the lab, propped against the large black lab table near the front of the room. The numbness had started in her feet. She looked at her arms. They seemed to be hers, except for her left hand, with the control fused to her skin.

She had jumped back too far. She had known there would be that risk. Tyler had said that when he went on trips longer than ten years he always felt depleted. But she had thought she could deal with depleted.

Her Now-self left the bench and walked over to Amelia. Her Now-self wore a ring on the third finger of her left hand. Had Amelia altered something by appearing? Or had she slipped into another life, another time? Had that trapped her?

Her Now-self's hands were shaking. They passed over Amelia's useless left hand, and her Now-self swallowed, hard. "Your control is broken," her Now-self said.

"I know," Amelia said.

But her Now-self was looking down and didn't seem to hear. Even in this place, she couldn't speak to herself.

Her Now-self set the control down. "Here," she said. "If I don't touch it, you can. Take mine."

Amelia shook her head. She couldn't move her arms. She smiled a little sadly. She would die here.

"You're the woman we saw all those years ago, aren't you?" Her Now-self asked.

Amelia nodded. She was getting too tired to speak.

"You went to see him, didn't you?" Her Now-self asked. "Just like I was going to."

Amelia smiled a little. She *had* seen him, one last time. And he had smiled at her. He loved her, no matter who or when she was.

"And it was wrong. It trapped you." Her Now-self stood. "When he—when he was alive, he made me promise to never come here by myself. He knew, didn't he?"

"He guessed," Amelia said, even though her Now-self couldn't hear.

"And all the precautions," her Now-self said quietly. "He was trying to protect me. He said, before he died, that he would always love me. And I didn't believe him. I had to see—"

Amelia nodded. The tingle filled her entire body. The light was returning, and the sound was fading. She had done this. She had made the changes, by appearing in her own past. As a ghost.

She wanted to tell her Now-self not to go, but she couldn't. She couldn't move at all.

**

THE LIGHT FADED ONE FINAL TIME. Amelia knew something supported her, but she couldn't feel it beneath the tingle in her body. As the red and green dots dissipated, she found herself on the four-poster bed in the adobe house, staring at the pictures on the wall.

They hadn't changed: she and Tyler gazing happily at each other, the baby between them; Tyler, giving away the bride. It took a moment before she understood what the photographs meant. They meant that her Now-self had heard, had understood. Her alternate self, the one who had married Tyler, born a child, and worked on the project, had set the controls aside, faced the dark and lonely house, and conquered it.

A breeze moved the curtains. The air had a fresh, salty smell here that she could have grown to love. A movement caught the corner of her eye. She tried to turn her head, but couldn't. The floorboards creaked, and the young woman in the white shift appeared at the edge of Amelia's vision.

"Grandmama," the woman said, kneeling beside the bed, "Grandmama, I miss you so."

Amelia smiled her last smile at the woman she and Tyler had helped make in a world she would never remember. "I missed you too, honey," she said as the light took her. "I missed you too."

Substitutions

SILAS SAT AT THE BLACKJACK TABLE, a plastic glass of whiskey in his left hand, and a small pile of hundred dollar chips in his right. His banjo rested against his boot, the embroidered strap wrapped around his calf. He had a pair of aces to the dealer's six, so he split them—a thousand dollars riding on each—and watched as she covered them with the expected tens.

He couldn't lose. He'd been trying to all night.

The casino was empty except for five gambling addicts hunkered over the blackjack table, one old woman playing slots with the rhythm of an assembly worker, and one young man in black leather who was getting drunk at the casino's sorry excuse for a bar. The employees showed no sign of holiday cheer: no happy holiday pins, no little Santa hats, only the stark black and white of their uniforms against the casino's fading glitter.

He had chosen the Paradise because it was one of the few remaining fifties-style casinos in Nevada, still thick with flocked wallpaper and cigarette smoke, craps tables worn by dice and elbows, and the roulette wheel creaking with age. It was also only a few hours from Reno, and in thirty hours, he would have to make the tortuous drive up there. Along the way, he would visit an old man who had a bad heart; a young girl who would cross the road at the wrong time and meet an on-coming semi; and a baby boy who was born with his lungs not yet fully formed. Silas also suspected a few surprises along the way; nothing was ever as it seemed any longer. Life was moving too fast, even for him.

But he had Christmas Eve and Christmas Day off, the two days he had chosen when he had been picked to work Nevada 150 years before. In those days, he would go home for Christmas, see his friends, spend time with his family. His parents welcomed him, even though they didn't see him for most of the year. He felt like a boy again, like someone cherished and loved, instead of the drifter he had become.

All of that stopped in 1878. December 26th, 1878. He wasn't yet sophisticated enough to know that the day was a holiday in England. Boxing Day. Not quite appropriate, but close.

He had to take his father that day. The old man had looked pale and tired throughout the holiday, but no one thought it serious. When he took to his bed Christmas night, everyone had simply thought him tired from the festivities.

It was only after midnight, when Silas got his orders, that he knew what was coming next. He begged off—

something he had never tried before (he wasn't even sure who he had been begging with)—but had received the feeling (that was all he ever got: a firm feeling, so strong he couldn't avoid it) that if he didn't do it, death would come another way—from Idaho or California or New Mexico. It would come another way, his father would be in agony for days, and the end, when it came, would be uglier than it had to be.

Silas had taken his banjo to the old man's room. His mother slept on her side, like she always had, her back to his father. His father's eyes had opened, and he knew. Somehow he knew.

They always did.

Silas couldn't remember what he said. Something—a bit of an apology, maybe, or just an explanation: *You always wanted to know what I did*. And then, the moment. First he touched his father's forehead, clammy with the illness that would claim him, and then Silas said, "You wanted to know why I carry the banjo," and strummed.

But the sound did not soothe his father like it had so many before him. As his spirit rose, his body struggled to hold it, and he looked at Silas with such a mix of fear and betrayal that Silas still saw it whenever he thought of his father.

The old man died, but not quickly and not easily, and Silas tried to resign, only to get sent to the place that passed for headquarters, a small shack that resembled an out-of-the-way railroad terminal. There, a man who looked no more than thirty but who had to be three hundred or more, told him the more that he complained, the longer his service would last.

Silas never complained again, and he had been on the job for 150 years. Almost 55,000 days spent in the service of Death, with only Christmas Eve and Christmas off, tainted holidays for a man in a tainted position.

He scooped up his winnings, piled them on his already-high stack of chips, and then placed his next bet. The dealer had just given him a queen and a jack when a boy sat down beside him.

"Boy" wasn't entirely accurate. He was old enough to get into the casino. But he had rain on his cheap jacket, and hair that hadn't been cut in a long time. IPod headphones stuck out of his breast pocket, and he had a cell phone against his hip the way that old sheriffs used to wear their guns.

His hands were callused and the nails had dirt beneath them. He looked tired, and a little frightened.

He watched as the dealer busted, then set chips in front of Silas and the four remaining players. Silas swept the chips into his stack, grabbed five of the hundred dollar chips, and placed the bet.

The dealer swept her hand along the semi-circle, silently asking the players to place their bets.

"You Silas?" the boy asked. He hadn't put any money on the table or placed any chips before him.

Silas sighed. Only once before had someone interrupted his Christmas festivities—if festivities was what the last century plus could be called.

The dealer peered at the boy. "You gonna play?"

The boy looked at her, startled. He didn't seem to know what to say.

"I got it." Silas put twenty dollars in chips in front of the boy.

"I don't know…"

"Just do what I tell you," Silas said.

The woman dealt, face-up. Silas got an ace. The boy, an eight. The woman dealt herself a ten. Then she went around again. Silas got his twenty-one—his weird holiday luck holding—but the boy got another eight.

"Split them," Silas said.

The boy looked at him, his fear almost palpable.

Silas sighed again, then grabbed another twenty in chips, and placed it next to the boy's first twenty.

"Jeez, mister, that's a lot of money," the boy whispered.

"Splitting," Silas said to the dealer.

She separated the cards and placed the bets behind them. Then she dealt the boy two cards—a ten and another eight.

The boy looked at Silas. Looked like the boy had peculiar luck as well.

"Split again," Silas said, more to the dealer than to the boy. He added the bet, let her separate the cards, and watched as she dealt the boy two more tens. Three eighteens. Not quite as good as Silas's twenties to twenty-ones, but just as statistically uncomfortable.

The dealer finished her round, then dealt herself a three, then a nine, busting again. She paid in order.

When she reached the boy, she set sixty dollars in chips before him, each in its own twenty dollar pile.

"Take it," Silas said.

"It's yours," the boy said, barely speaking above a whisper.

"I gave it to you."

"I don't gamble," the boy said.

"Well, for someone who doesn't gamble, you did pretty well. Take your winnings."

The boy looked at them as if they'd bite him. "I…"

"Are you leaving them for the next round?" the dealer asked.

The boy's eyes widened. He was clearly horrified at the very thought. With shaking fingers, he collected the chips, then leaned into Silas. The boy smelled of sweat and wet wool.

"Can I talk to you?" he whispered.

Silas nodded, then cashed in his chips. He'd racked up ten thousand dollars in three hours. He wasn't even having fun at it any more. He liked losing, felt that it was appropriate—part of the game, part of his life—but the losses had become fewer and farther between the more he played.

The more he lived. A hundred years ago, there were women and a few adopted children. But watching them grow old, helping three of them die, had taken the desire out of that too.

"Mr. Silas," the boy whispered.

"If you're not going to bet," the dealer said, "please move so someone can have your seats."

People had gathered behind Silas, and he hadn't even noticed. He really didn't care tonight. Normally, he would have noticed anyone around him—noticed who they were, how and when they would die.

"Come on," he said, gathering the bills the dealer had given him. The boy's eyes went to the money like a hungry man's went to food. His one-hundred-and-twenty dollars remained on the table, and Silas had to remind him to pick it up.

The boy used a forefinger and a thumb to carry it, as if it would burn him.

"At least put it in your pocket," Silas snapped.

"But it's yours," the boy said.

"It's a damn gift. Appreciate it."

The boy blinked, then stuffed the money into the front of his unwashed jeans. Silas led him around banks and banks of slot machines, all pinging and ponging and making little musical come-ons, to the steakhouse in the back.

The steakhouse was the reason Silas came back year after year. The place opened at five, closed at three a.m., and served the best steaks in Vegas. They weren't arty or too small. One big slab of meat, expensive cut, charred on the outside and red as Christmas on the inside. Beside the steak they served french-fried onions, and sides that no self-respecting Strip restaurant would prepare—creamed corn, au gratin potatoes, popovers—the kind of stuff that Silas always associated with the modern Las Vegas—modern, to him, meaning 1950s-1960s Vegas. Sin city. A place for grown-ups to gamble and smoke and drink and have affairs. The Vegas of Sinatra and the mob, not the Vegas of Steve Wynn and his ilk, who prettified everything and made it all seem upscale and oh-so-right.

Silas still worked Vegas a lot more than any other Nevada city, which made sense, considering how many millions of people lived there now, but millions of people lived all over. Even sparsely populated Nevada, one of the least populated states in the Union, had ten full-time Death employees. They tried to unionize a few years ago, but Silas, with the most seniority, refused to join. Then they tried to limit the routes—one would get Reno, another Sparks, another Elko and that region, and a few would split Vegas—but Silas wouldn't agree to that either.

He loved the travel part of the job. It was the only part he still liked, the ability to go from place to place to place, see the changes, understand how time affected everything.

Everything except him.

The maitre d sat them in the back, probably because of the boy. Even in this modern era, where people wore blue jeans to funerals, this steakhouse preferred its customers in a suit and tie.

The booth was made of wood and rose so high that Silas couldn't see anything but the boy and the table across from them. A single lamp reflected against the wall, revealing cloth napkins and real silver utensils.

The boy stared at them with the same kind of fear he had shown at the blackjack table. "I can't—."

The maître d gave them leather-bound menus, said something about a special, and then handed Silas a wine list. Silas ordered a bottle of burgundy. He didn't know a lot about wines, just that the more expensive ones tasted a lot better than the rest of them. So he ordered the most expensive burgundy on the menu.

The maître d nodded crisply, almost militarily, and then left. The boy leaned forward.

"I can't stay. I'm your substitute."

Silas smiled. A waiter came by with a bread basket—hard rolls, still warm—and relish trays filled with sliced carrots, celery, and radishes, and candied beets, things people now would call old-fashioned.

Modern, to him. Just as modern as always.

The boy squirmed, his jeans squeaking on the leather booth.

"I know," Silas said. "You'll be fine."

"I got—

"A big one, probably," Silas said. "It's Christmas Eve. Traffic, right? A shooting in a church? Too many suicides?"

"No," the boy said, distressed. "Not like that."

"When's it scheduled for?" Silas asked. He really wanted his dinner, and he didn't mind sharing it. The boy looked like he needed a good meal.

"Tonight," the boy said. "No specific time. See?"

He put a crumpled piece of paper between them, but Silas didn't pick it up.

"Means you have until midnight," Silas said. "It's only seven. You can eat."

"They said at orientation—

Silas had forgotten; they all got orientation now. The expectations of generations. He'd been thrown into the pool feet first, fumbling his way for six months before someone told him that he could actually ask questions.

"—the longer you wait, the more they suffer."

Silas glanced at the paper. "If it's big, it's a surprise. They won't suffer. They'll just finish when you get there. That's all."

The boy bit his lip. "How do you know?"

Because he'd had big. He'd had grisly. He'd had disgusting. He'd overseen more deaths than the boy could imagine.

The head waiter arrived, took Silas's order, and then turned to the boy.

"I don't got money," the boy said.

"You have one-hundred-and-twenty dollars," Silas said. "But I'm buying, so don't worry."

The boy opened the menu, saw the prices, and closed it again. He shook his head.

The waiter started to leave when Silas stopped him. "Give him what I'm having. Medium well."

Since the kid didn't look like he ate many steaks, he wouldn't like his rare. Rare was an acquired taste, just like burgundy wine and the cigar that Silas wished he could light up. Not everything in the modern era was an improvement.

"You don't have to keep paying for me," the kid said.

Silas waved the waiter away, then leaned back. The back of the booth, made of wood, was rigid against his spine. "After a while in this business," he said, "money is all you have."

The kid bit his lower lip. "Look at the paper. Make sure I'm not screwing up. Please."

But Silas didn't look.

"You're supposed to handle all of this on your own," Silas said gently.

"I know," the boy said. "I know. But this one, he's scary. And I don't think anything I do will make it right."

***

AFTER HE FINISHED HIS STEAK and had his first sip of coffee, about the time he would have lit up his cigar, Silas picked up the paper. The boy had devoured the steak like he hadn't eaten in weeks. He ate all the bread and everything from his relish tray.

He was very, very new.

Silas wondered how someone that young had gotten into the death business, but he was determined not to ask. It would be some variation on his own story. Silas had begged for the life of his wife who should have died in the delivery of their second child. Begged, and begged, and begged, and somehow, in his befogged state, he actually saw the woman whom he then called the Angel of Death.

Now he knew better—none of them were angels, just working stiffs waiting for retirement—but then, she had seemed perfect and terrifying, all at the same time.

He'd asked for his wife, saying he didn't want to raise his daughters alone.

The angel had tilted her head. "Would you die for her?"

"Of course," Silas said.

"Leaving her to raise the children alone?" the angel asked.

His breath caught. "Is that my only choice?"

She shrugged, as if she didn't care. Later, when he reflected, he realized she didn't know.

"Yes," he said into her silence. "She would raise better people than I will. She's good. I'm...not."

He wasn't bad, he later realized, just lost, as so many were. His wife had been a god-fearing woman with strict ideas about morality. She had raised two marvelous girls, who became two strong women, mothers of large broods who all went on to do good works.

In that, he hadn't been wrong.

But his wife hadn't remarried either, and she had cried for him for the rest of her days.

They had lived in Texas. He had made his bargain, got assigned Nevada, and had to swear never to head east, not while his wife and children lived. His parents saw him, but they couldn't tell anyone. They thought he ran out on his wife and children, and oddly, they had supported him in it.

Remnants of his family still lived. Great-grandchildren generations removed. He still couldn't head east, and he no longer wanted to.

Silas touched the paper and it burned his fingers. A sign, a warning, a remembrance that he wasn't supposed to work these two days.

Two days out of an entire year.

He slid the paper back to the boy. "I can't open it. I'm not allowed. You tell me."

So the boy did.

And Silas, in wonderment that they had sent a rookie into a situation a veteran might not be able to handle, settled his tab, took the boy by the arm, and led him into the night.

***

EVERY CITY HAS POCKETS OF EVIL. Vegas had fewer than most, despite the things the television lied about. So many people worked in law enforcement or security, so many others were bonded so that they could work in casinos or high-end jewelry stores or banks that Vegas's serious crime was lower than most comparable cities of its size.

Silas appreciated that. Most of the time, it meant that the deaths he attended in Vegas were natural or easy or just plain silly. He got a lot of silly deaths in that city. Some he even found time to laugh over.

But not this one.

As they drove from the very edge of town, past the rows and rows of similar houses, past the stink and desperation of complete poverty, he finally asked, "How long've you been doing this?"

"Six months," the boy said softly, as if that were forever.

Silas looked at him, looked at the young face reflecting the Christmas lights that filled the neighborhood, and shook his head. "All substitutes?"

The boy shrugged. "They didn't have any open routes."

"What about the guy you replaced?"

"He'd been subbing, waiting to retire. They say you could retire too, but you show no signs of it. Working too hard, even for a younger man."

He wasn't older. He was the same age he had been when his wife struggled with her labor—a breach birth that would be no problem in 2006, but had been deadly if not handled right in 1856. The midwife's hands hadn't been clean—not that anyone knew better in those days—and the infection had started even before the baby got turned.

He shuddered, that night alive in him. The night he'd made his bargain.

"I don't work hard," he said. "I work less than I did when I started."

The boy looked at him, surprised. "Why don't you retire?"

"And do what?" Silas asked. He hadn't planned to speak up. He normally shrugged off that question.

"I dunno," the boy said. "Relax. Live off your savings. Have a family again."

They could all have families again when they retired. Families and a good, rich life, albeit short. Silas would age when he retired. He would age and have no special powers. He would watch a new wife die in childbirth and not be able to see his former colleague sitting beside the bed. He would watch his children squirm after a car accident, blood on their faces, knowing that they would live poorly if they lived at all, and not be able to find out the future from the death dealer hovering near the scene.

Better to continue. Better to keep this half-life, this half-future, time without end.

"Families are overrated," Silas said. They look at you with betrayal and loss when you do what was right.

But the boy didn't know that yet. He didn't know a lot.

"You ever get scared?" the boy asked.

"Of what?" Silas asked. Then gave the standard answer. "They can't kill you. They can't harm you. You just move from place to place, doing your job. There's nothing to be scared of."

The boy grunted, sighed, and looked out the window.

Silas knew what he had asked, and hadn't answered it. Of course he got scared. All the time. And not of dying—even though he still wasn't sure what happened to the souls he freed. He wasn't scared of that, or of the people he occasionally faced down, the drug addicts with their knives, the gangsters with their guns, the wannabe outlaws with blood all over their hands.

No, the boy had asked about the one thing to be afraid of, the one thing they couldn't change.

Was he scared of being alone? Of remaining alone, for the rest of his days? Was he scared of being unknown and nearly invisible, having no ties and no dreams?

It was too late to be scared of that.

He'd lived it. He lived it every single day.

***

THE HOUSE WAS ONE OF THOSE SQUARE adobe things that filled Vegas. It was probably pink in the sunlight. In the half-light that passed for nighttime in this perpetually alive city, it looked gray and foreboding.

The bars on the windows—standard in this neighborhood—didn't help.

Places like this always astounded him. They seemed so normal, so incorruptible, just another building on another street, like all the other buildings on all the other streets. Sometimes he got to go into those buildings. Very few of them were different from what he expected. Oh, the art changed or the furniture. The smells differed—sometimes unwashed diapers, sometimes perfume, sometimes the heavy scent of meals eaten long ago—but the rest remained the same: the television in the main room, the kitchen with its square table (sometimes decorated with flowers, sometimes nothing but trash), the double bed in the second bedroom down the hall, the one with its own shower and toilet. The room across from the main bathroom was sometimes an office, sometimes a den, sometimes a child's bedroom. If it was a child's bedroom, there were pictures on the wall, studio portraits from the local mall, done up in cheap frames, showing the passing years. The pictures were never straight, and always dusty, except for the most recent, hung with pride in the only remaining empty space.

He had a hunch this house would have none of those things. If anything, it would have an overly neat interior. The television would be in the kitchen or the bedroom or both. The front room would have a sofa set designed for looks, not for comfort. And one of the rooms would be blocked off, maybe even marked private, and in it, he would find (if he looked) trophies of a kind that made even his cast-iron stomach turn.

These houses had no attic. Most didn't have a basement. So the scene would be the garage. The car would be parked outside of it, blocking the door, and the neighbors would assume that the garage was simply a workspace—not that far off, if the truth be told.

He'd been to places like this before. More times than he wanted to think about, especially in the smaller communities out in the desert, the communities that had no names, or once had a name and did no longer. The communities sometimes made up of cheap trailers and empty storefronts, with a whorehouse a few miles off the main highway, and a casino in the center of town, a casino so old it made the one that the boy found him in look like it had been built just the week before.

He hated these jobs. He wasn't sure what made him come with the boy. A moment of compassion? The prospect of yet another long Christmas Eve with nothing to punctuate it except the bong-bong of nearby slots?

He couldn't go to church any more. It didn't feel right, with as many lives as he had taken. He couldn't go to church or listen to the singing or look at the families and wonder which of them he'd be standing beside in thirty years.

Maybe he belonged here more than the boy did. Maybe he belonged here more than anyone else.

They parked a block away, not because anyone would see their car—if asked, hours later, the neighbors would deny seeing anything to do with Silas or the boy. Maybe they never saw, maybe their memories vanished. Silas had never been clear on that either.

As they got out, Silas asked, "What do you use?"

The boy reached into the breast pocket. For a moment, Silas thought he'd remove the iPod, and Silas wasn't sure how a device that used headphones would work. Then the boy removed a harmonica—expensive, the kind sold at high-end music stores.

"You play that before all this?" Silas asked.

The boy nodded. "They got me a better one, though."

Silas's banjo had been all his own. They'd let him take it, and nothing else. The banjo, the clothes he wore that night, his hat.

He had different clothes now. He never wore a hat. But his banjo was the same as it had always been—new and pure with a sound that he still loved.

It was in the trunk. He doubted it could get stolen, but he took precautions just in case.

He couldn't bring it on this job. This wasn't his job. He'd learned the hard way that the banjo didn't work except in assigned cases. When he'd wanted to help, to put someone out of their misery, to step in where another death dealer had failed, he couldn't. He could only watch, like normal people did, and hope that things got better, even though he knew it wouldn't.

The boy clutched the harmonica in his right hand. The dry desert air was cold. Silas could see his breath. The tourists down on the Strip, with their short skirts and short sleeves, probably felt betrayed by the normal winter chill. He wished he were there with them, instead of walking through this quiet neighborhood, filled with dark houses, dirt-ridden yards, and silence.

So much silence. You'd think there'd be at least one barking dog.

When they reached the house, the boy headed to the garage, just like Silas expected. A car was parked on the road—a 1980s sedan that looked like it had seen better days. In the driveway, a brand-new van with tinted windows, custom-made for bad deeds.

In spite of himself, Silas shuddered.

The boy stopped outside and steeled himself, then he looked at Silas with sadness in his eyes. Silas nodded. The boy extended a hand—Silas couldn't get in without the boy's momentary magic—and then they were inside, near the stench of old gasoline, urine, and fear.

The kids sat in a dimly lit corner, chained together like the slaves on ships in the 19th century. The windows were covered with dirty cardboard, the concrete floor was empty except for stains as old as time. It felt bad in here, a recognizable bad, one Silas had encountered before.

The boy was shaking. He wasn't out of place here, his old wool jacket and his dirty jeans making him a cousin to the kids on the floor. Silas had a momentary flash: they were homeless. Runaways, lost, children without borders, without someone looking for them.

"You've been here before," Silas whispered to the boy and the boy's eyes filled with tears.

Been here, negotiated here, moved on here—didn't quite die, but no longer quite lived—and for who? A group of kids like this one? A group that had somehow escaped, but hadn't reported what had happened?

Then he felt the chill grow worse. Of course they hadn't reported it. Who would believe them? A neat homeowner kidnaps a group of homeless kids for his own personal playthings, and the cops believe the kids? Kids who steal and sell drugs and themselves just for survival.

People like the one who owned this house were cautious. They were smart. They rarely got caught unless they went public with letters or phone calls or both.

They had to prepare for contingencies like losing a plaything now and then. They probably had all the answers planned.

A side door opened. It was attached to the house. The man who came in was everything Silas had expected—white, thin, balding, a bit too intense.

What surprised Silas was the look the man gave him. Measuring, calculating.

Pleased.

The man wasn't supposed to see Silas or the boy. Not until the last moment.

Not until the end.

Silas had heard that some of these creatures could see the death dealers. A few of Silas's colleagues speculated that these men continued to kill so that they could continue to see death in all its forms, collecting images the way they collected trophies.

After seeing the momentary victory in that man's eyes, Silas believed it.

The man picked up the kid at the end of the chain. Too weak to stand, the kid staggered a bit, then had to lean into the man.

"You have to beat me," the man said to Silas. "I slice her first, and you have to leave."

The boy was still shivering. The man hadn't noticed him. The man thought Silas was here for him, not the boy. Silas had no powers, except the ones that humans normally had—not on this night, and not in this way.

If he were here alone, he'd start playing, and praying he'd get the right one. If there was a right one. He couldn't tell. They all seemed to have the mark of death over them.

No wonder the boy needed him.

It was a fluid situation, one that could go in any direction.

"Start playing," Silas said under his breath.

But the man heard him, not the boy. The man pulled the kid's head back, exposing a smooth white throat with the heartbeat visible in a vein.

"Play!" Silas shouted, and ran forward, shoving the man aside, hoping that would be enough.

It saved the girl's neck, for a moment anyway. She fell, and landed on the other kid next to her. The kid moved away, as if proximity to her would cause the kid to die.

The boy started blowing on his harmonica. The notes were faint, barely notes, more like bleats of terror.

The man laughed. He saw the boy now. "So you're back to rob me again," he said.

The boy's playing grew wispier.

"Ignore him," Silas said to the boy.

"Who're you? His coach?" The man approached him. "I know your rules. I destroy you, I get to take your place."

The steak rolled in Silas's stomach. The man was half right. He destroyed Silas, and he would get a chance to take the job. He destroyed both of them, and he would get the job, by old magic not new. Silas had forgotten this danger. No wonder these creatures liked to see death—what better for them than to be the facilitator for the hundreds of people who died in Nevada every day.

The man brandished his knife. "Lessee," he said. "What do I do? Destroy the instrument, deface the man. Right? And send him to hell."

Get him fired, Silas fought. It wasn't really hell, although it seemed like it. He became a ghost, existing forever, but not allowed to interact with anything. He was fired. He lost the right to die.

The man reached for the harmonica. Silas shoved again.

"Play!" Silas shouted.

And miraculously, the boy played. "Home on the Range," a silly song for these circumstances, but probably the first tune the boy had ever learned. He played it with spirit as he backed away from the fight.

But the kids weren't rebelling. They sat on the cold concrete floor, already half dead, probably tortured into submission. If they didn't rise up and kill this monster, no one would.

Silas looked at the boy. Tears streamed down his face, and he nodded toward the kids. Souls hovered above them, as if they couldn't decide whether or not to leave.

Damn the ones in charge: they'd sent the kid here as his final test. Could he take the kind of lives he had given his life for? Was he that strong?

The man reached for the harmonica again, and this time Silas grabbed his knife. It was heavier than Silas expected. He had never wielded a real instrument of death. His banjo eased people into forever. It didn't force them out of their lives a moment too early.

The boy kept playing and the man—the creature—laughed. One of the kids looked up, and Silas thought the kid was staring straight at the boy.

Only a moment, then. Only a moment to decide.

Silas shoved the knife into the man's belly. It went in deep, and the man let out an oof of pain. He stumbled, reached for the knife, and then glared at Silas.

Silas hadn't killed him, maybe hadn't even mortally wounded him. No soul appeared above him, and even these creatures had souls—dark and tainted as they were.

The boy's playing broke in places as if he were trying to catch his breath. The kid at the end of the chain, the girl, managed to get up. She looked at the knife, then at the man, then around the room. She couldn't see Silas or the boy.

Which was good.

The man was pulling on the knife. He would get it free in a moment. He would use it, would destroy these children, the ones no one cared about except the boy who was here to take their souls.

The girl kicked the kid beside her. "Stand up," she said.

The kid looked at her, bleary. Silas couldn't tell if these kids were male or female. He wasn't sure it mattered.

"Stand up," the girl said again.

In a rattle of chains, the kid did. The man didn't notice. He was working the knife, grunting as he tried to dislodge it. Silas stepped back, wondering if he had already interfered too much.

The music got louder, more intense, almost violent. The girl stood beside the man and stared at him for a moment.

He raised his head, saw her, and grinned.

Then she reached down with that chain, wrapped it around his neck and pulled. "Help me," she said to the others. "Help me."

The music became a live thing, wrapping them all, filling the smelly garage, and reaching deep, deep into the darkness. The soul did rise up—half a soul, broken and burned. It looked at Silas, then flared at the boy, who—bless him—didn't stop playing.

Then the soul floated toward the growing darkness in the corner, a blackness Silas had seen only a handful of times before, a blackness that felt as cold and dark as any empty desert night, and somehow much more permanent.

The music faded. The girl kept pulling, until another kid, farther down the line, convinced her to let go.

"We have to find the key," the other kid—a boy—said.

"On the wall," a third kid said. "Behind the electric box."

They shuffled as a group toward the box. They walked through Silas, and he felt them, alive and vibrant. For a moment, he worried that he had been fired, but he knew he had too many years for that. Too many years of perfect service—and he hadn't killed the man. He had just injured him, took away the threat to the boy.

That was allowed, just barely.

No wonder the boy had brought him. No wonder the boy had asked him if he was scared. Not of being alone or being lonely. But of certain jobs, of the things now asked of them as the no-longer-quite-human beings that they were.

Silas turned to the boy. His face was shiny with tears, but his eyes were clear. He stuffed the harmonica back into his breast pocket.

"You knew he'd beat you without me," Silas said.

The boy nodded.

"You knew this wasn't a substitution. You would have had this job, even without me."

"It's not cheating to bring in help," the boy said.

"But it's nearly impossible to find it," Silas said. "How did you find me?"

"It's Christmas Eve," the boy said. "Everyone knows where you'd be."

Everyone. His colleagues. People on the job. The only folks who even knew his name any more.

Silas sighed. The boy reached out with his stubby dirty hand. Silas took it, and then, suddenly, they were out of that fetid garage. They stood next to the van and watched as the cardboard came off one of the windows, as glass shattered outward.

Kids, homeless kids, injured and alone, poured out of that window like water.

"Thanks," the boy said. "I can't tell you how much it means."

But Silas knew. The boy didn't yet, but Silas did. When he retired—no longer if. When—this boy would see him again. This boy would take him, gently and with some kind of majestic harmonica music, to a beyond Silas could not imagine.

The boy waved at him, and joined the kids, heading into the dark Vegas night. Those kids couldn't see him, but they had to know he was there, like a guardian angel, saving them from horrors that would haunt their dreams for the rest of their lives.

Silas watched them go. Then he headed in the opposite direction, toward his car. What had those kids seen? The man—the creature—with his knife out, raving at nothing. Then stumbling backwards, once, twice, the second time with a knife in his belly. They'd think that he tripped, that he stabbed himself. None of them had seen Silas or the boy.

They wouldn't for another sixty years.

If they were lucky.

The neighborhood remained dark, although a dog barked in the distance. His car was cold. Cold and empty.

He let himself in, started it, warmed his fingers against the still-hot air blowing out of the vents. Only a few minutes gone. A few minutes to take away a nasty, horrible lifetime. He wondered what was in the rest of these houses, and hoped he'd never have to find out.

The clock on the dash read 10:45. As he drove out of the neighborhood, he passed a small adobe church. Outside, candles burned in candleholders made of baked sand. Almost like the churches of his childhood.

Almost, but not quite.

He watched the people thread inside. They wore fancy clothing—dresses on the women, suits on the men, the children dressing like their parents, faces alive with anticipation.

They believed in something.

They had hope.

He wondered if hope was something a man could recapture, if it came with time, relaxation, and the slow inevitable march toward death.

He wondered, if he retired, whether he could spend his Christmas Eves inside, smelling the mix of incense and candle wax, the evergreen boughs, and the light dusting of ladies' perfume.

He wondered…

Then shook his head.

And drove back to the casino, to spend the rest of his time off in peace.

Snow Angels

So GRAMPS TOOK THEM DOWN to the road anyway. Bobberts stuck his hands in his pockets. His fingers found his dad's Swiss Army knife. He didn't even get to use it. Dad was kinda mean about that.

You don't use knives to cut trees, Bobs, Dad said. *That's what the chainsaw is for.*

But Bobberts brought the knife so they wouldn't need the chainsaw. Last year, Daddy said the chainsaw was why Gramps took Bobberts and Sarah to the car before the Christmas tree was cut.

Too much could go wrong with chainsaws.

So him and Sarah got sent to the car again. This time, Bobberts was mad.

Sarah didn't care. She just skipped ahead, happy to be in the trees and the snow. She liked outside, she liked playing, she liked it all.

She didn't know there was cool stuff they couldn't do.

Dad said Bobberts would get to do it "some day."

Bobberts was beginning to think "some day" meant "never."

The snow on the path was muddy. You could see the rocks underneath it. Bobberts kicked one, and Gramps laughed.

"It's not that much fun, kiddo," Gramps said. "They get a chainsaw and just slice through the tree. It's over in five seconds."

Bobberts nodded. Dad said the same thing, but that didn't mean it was true. Bobbert'd never seen somebody use a chainsaw—Dad said he was too little. He was nine now, and tall for his age. Everybody said so.

He wasn't little any more.

Sarah skipped through the trees. "There's the car," she said, pointing.

Their car and two others. Those weirdo people who were walking with Daddy and the tree guy into the woods. Bobberts didn't want to call it a farm, because he didn't see pigs and cows and horses. It was just a woods with lots of Christmas trees.

Gramps reached the car first, and unlocked it. Then he rubbed his hands together. "You kids get inside," he said. "I gotta see a man about a dog."

As he walked back up the path, Sarah looked at Bobbert. "There's dogs?" she asked.

Bobberts shook his head. "Gramps says that when he's gotta go Number One."

Sarah giggled and put her hands over her mouth. She was still little. Four. Mom said everybody had to watch out for her. Small and pretty and all girl, that's what Mom said. But Mom never saw the goofy side of Sarah, except that one time. That time she was really, really little and trying to learn Bobberts' name. She couldn't say Bobbie, so Daddy tried to teach her Robert.

It came out Bobberts, and it stuck.

Sometimes Bobberts liked it. Sometimes he wished she wasn't so cute so everybody remembered everything she said.

She took his hand and tugged. "Lookie the snow."

She pointed at the field above the cars. The trees didn't start right away. There was one big pile of white.

He knew what she was thinking. Sarah'd been like this ever since the snow started. One big pile of white and she wanted to dive in it.

Finally Daddy taught her snow angels just so she wouldn't go running into the big pile of white and dive into a rock or something.

"Don't wanna," Bobberts said. He'd get colder than he already was. Besides, big kids didn't make snow angels.

"C'mon." Sarah tugged him toward the empty whiteness. Bobberts looked around for Gramps, but didn't see him. The trees were pretty thin right near the road.

Gramps taught Bobberts how to pee in the woods last year.

First rule, Gramps had said, *go deep enough that no-body can see you.*

A car went by on the road, kicking up slush. Bob-berts winced. He was gonna get wet and cold no matter where he was.

"You do it," he said.

Sarah stuck her tongue out at him, and ran up the hill. She stopped smack in the middle, turned to face the road, spread her arms, and fell backwards.

Snow puffed up around her.

Bobberts kicked the snow off a nearby rock and perched on it. He could see Sarah and he could see the path. Far away, he heard the moan of a chainsaw, and closer, the slam of a car door.

Sarah made a perfect angel. Then she sat up, and wiped the snow off her face. "C'*mon*," she said.

Bobberts shook his head.

She put her thumb to her nose and waggled her fingers at him. Then she got up, moved a few steps down, and flopped again.

How many snow angels was she gonna make?

Mom would be so mad at him. Sarah wasn't wearing her mittens, and her coat was gonna get soaked.

Bobberts looked up the trail for Gramps, but still didn't see him. Then something caught his eye. A guy was standing in the thin trees, staring down at Sarah. The guy was wearing gray, just like the trees, and he blended into the hillside.

Bobberts felt a little shiver. How long had that guy been there?

Adults were so creepy.

Sarah sat up again, took off her hat, and shook snow from it. Then she stuck it on her blonde curls. This time she didn't look at Bobberts at all.

This time, she went farther down the hill.

He saw the pattern she was making. Snow angels, like those cutouts you make with folded papers and scissors. She was really good at stuff like that. Mom said Sarah was gonna be an artist one day.

Bobberts sighed. This was taking forever. Daddy said only five minutes and it had to be lots more than that. The chainsaw still rumbled back there.

The tree wasn't even that great. There was a bigger, fuller one right next to it, but Daddy said it wouldn't fit in the front door. Gramps'd winked at Bobberts and said Daddy just didn't want to carry it all the way back to the car.

Bobberts rubbed his nose with the back of his hand. He was getting snow snot. Nose drips that happened out in the cold, that's what snow snot was. Gramps said so. Sarah said it was just icky, and Bobberts agreed.

Sarah.

He looked up. She was in the middle of her fourth angel. She'd done 'em so perfect that they looked like they were hanging along the slope. She'd fallen on her own footprints, so you couldn't see them at all.

Then that guy came out of the trees. He snuck out, like he didn't want nobody to see him. He walked right into the middle of the fourth angel, screwing it all up, and bent down.

Sarah screamed.

Bobberts stood up. No Gramps. Nobody, just that chainsaw still whirring far away.

The man grabbed Sarah by her arms and pulled her up. She was screaming and kicking and biting just like Mom taught them to do.

The man didn't care. He just grabbed her like Daddy did sometimes, and tucked her under his arm. She was yelling, "Bobberts! Bobberts!"

And Bobberts didn't know what to do.

The man was going back toward the trees.

Bobberts looked at the path, but it was empty. He bit his lower lip, and headed up the hillside.

When someone gets you, Mom always said, *you do what you gotta do to get away.*

She never said what you gotta to do when someone got Sarah.

Bobberts was breathing hard. He had to hurry. That guy had Sarah and she was screaming and he was scared—what if that guy was one of those guys who hurt little kids? What if they never see Sarah again?

Bobberts could hear himself breathe. It sounded louder than the screaming, louder than that weird saw noise. Louder than the guy yelling at Sarah to shut up.

But the guy had his back to Bobberts, and he was hurrying.

Through the trees, Bobberts could see the car. It was the same one that had passed earlier, the one that sent slush everywhere.

The guy'd seen Sarah and come back for her.

That made Bobberts even madder.

They were almost at the trees. Bobberts had to do something.

He ran the last few steps, slipping on the snow. And that's when he thought of it: He was wearing really good boots (Mom made him) but that guy was wearing Nikes.

Nikes weren't made for snow.

Bobberts reached the guy and grabbed the guy's back leg. The guy's front foot slipped. The guy turned and yanked at the same time, sliding on the snow. Bobberts let go.

The guy fell on his belly, and went down the hill like he was on a sled, dropping Sarah. She was crying really hard now. The fall had hurt her too.

Bobberts half ran, half slid down near them.

"Sarah!" Bobberts yelled. "Run away!"

Sarah was stretched out in the snow. She was still crying. Sometimes she could cry so hard she'd forget what she was doing.

Bobberts pointed to the path. "Get Gramps!"

She stumbled. The guy crawled toward her, getting close to Bobberts.

And that's when Bobberts kicked him.

The guy rolled onto his back. He was really big and really mean-looking. Bobberts was never so scared in his whole life, not even when the sixth grade boys ganged up on him.

"Boy or girl," the man said in an icky voice. "Don't matter to me."

He pulled Bobberts to him, but didn't knock Bobberts down.

The guy grinned at him, and a shiver went through Bobberts. A shiver, and an ick, and a fear like he'd never had.

So he kicked again. Kicked and kicked in the place Gramps said no boy ever really liked, and the man was squealing and rolling away and holding himself, and Sarah was gone—where'd she go?—and there wasn't sound, except Bobberts' breathing and the guy squealing and the bam of Bobberts' boot hitting the guy.

Then the guy's hand grabbed Bobberts' foot, and Bobberts went down, just like Sarah did when she was making snow angels. Only he was surprised and the air went right out of his body.

"Don't make no difference." The man's voice sounded airy now, and kinda weird. He sat up. His skin was sickly looking, like he was gonna puke.

The guy was bigger than the sixth-grade boys and Bobberts couldn't stop them from beating him up. This guy would win. This guy would hurt him.

But Momma said when someone gets you, you do what you gotta do to get away.

Bobberts slipped his hand in his pocket. Daddy was already mad at him about the knife. He told Bobberts that Bobberts was too young to use it.

Do what you can, Momma whispered in his ear.

Bobberts dug the knife out, and snicked it open and jabbed it in the guy's arm. The guy screamed and reached for the knife, but Bobberts remembered to pull it out so that Daddy wouldn't get mad that it got stolen, and the guy was calling Bobberts bad names, and pulling even harder on Bobberts' boot, and Bobberts stabbed the guy's arm again, and again, and then Bobberts missed, and the knife slipped and hit the guy in the leg.

The guy really screamed, and far away, Bobberts heard Gramps yelling his name, then yelling for Daddy, and then just yelling.

But the guy was screaming and rolling away from Bobberts and blood was squirting like the guy's leg was one giant water pistol, and snow was getting all red.

The guy'd let go of Bobberts' ankle, but it took him a minute to tell because his ankle still hurt. His whole body hurt from falling and running out of air, and the guy was still screaming, and Daddy was yelling now, and Bobberts got up and tripped his way over Sarah's snow angels to the path.

Gramps took his arm, and Daddy was running down from the woods, and Sarah was crying, and the tree guy was yelling into his phone about police and help and the weirdo couple behind him wanted to use the chainsaw to scare the guy, and Gramps said it wouldn't be necessary because he'd be dead soon anyway.

And at first Bobberts thought Gramps meant the guy would be dead because Gramps would see to it, but Gramps didn't mean that at all. The guy had stopped screaming and the blood wasn't squirting any more, and the snow was so red it didn't look like snow, and the blood was dripping down the footprints into Sarah's snow angels, decorating them like Momma decorated her Christmas cookies, with a touch of red over the white.

Then Daddy reached them and grabbed Sarah and looked at Bobberts and Gramps said, "The kid saved them both," and Daddy looked like he was gonna cry, and Bobberts knew exactly why.

He held out the knife. It was bent funny and covered with gunk. He said, "I'm sorry, Daddy. I think I broke it."

And Daddy took the knife from him, dropped it onto the path, and pulled Bobberts to his other side.

Bobberts clung onto Daddy's jeans, feeling Daddy's leg shake, or maybe Bobberts was shaking, and Sarah was crying, and Gramps was telling everybody to stay on the path, and Daddy said, "It's okay," but they all knew it really wasn't.

The tree guy couldn't wait and he had to go see if the mean guy was all right, and Gramps kept shaking his head. Bobberts wanted to get out of there, but he knew they couldn't go yet.

"Daddy," Bobberts said. "You forgot the tree."

And Daddy laughed, only it didn't sound like a Daddy-laugh. It sounded kinda shaky and weird, and he looked at Gramps, and he said, "I think we're gonna get a tree from the store," and Bobberts didn't know what that meant, but he nodded anyway.

Sarah wiped her face off, and lifted her head, and said, "I was just making angels, Daddy."

"I know," Daddy said. "I know. And they protected you, honey."

"Uh-uh," Sarah said. "That was Bobberts."

And Bobberts smiled, even though he was shaking. He smiled and reached for his sister, and hugged her, even though it was a baby thing to do.

And nobody said nothing, nobody except Gramps, who said, "We got hot cocoa in the car," like it was a reward.

And maybe it was.

Like smiling against his dad's leg, and hugging his sister, and being really, really glad that nobody said nothing about the knife, lying bloody and broken in the snow.

The Taste of Miracles

HAYES STARED AT THE VASTNESS of space through the freighter's window. He swiveled slightly in the pilot's chair, wincing as he banged his knees on the control panel. No matter how many times he did this run, the sight fascinated him. Even the blackness looked crisp, and the points of light appeared sharp. Thousands of stars. Thousands of possibilities.

Trish brushed his shoulder. He turned, and she handed him a steaming mug. "Cocoa," she said.

He took it, feeling the heat through the durable plastic. "I didn't know we had chocolate aboard."

She smiled and eased in the chair next to his. She was as slim and battered as the freighter, her skin lined with the effort from all the years of hauling, lifting, and loading. He had called her scrappy until he had seen her in a fight with one of the ore miners in the bar at the ass-end of the moon base. After that, Hayes decided, "tough" was too wimpy a word for Trish.

"Needed a little something special tonight," she said, then blew gently at the steam.

He glanced at her, her small, strong hands wrapped around the mug as if it would give her warmth. "Didn't think you celebrated holidays."

Her grin was tiny. She didn't look at him. "Don't. Not really, anyway. But I kinda like this run on Christmas."

Earth to the Moon and back. One of the easiest runs on the freight line. He preferred Earth to Mars because he liked Mars better. It stirred his imagination in a way the Moon never did. "I like it too," he said. "Pays triple."

"No. I don't care about that." She slurped. The entire area smelled of hot chocolate. "You celebrate Christmas, Hayes?"

"I'm not religious," he said.

"I mean as a kid. You get to celebrate? Tree and tinsel and toys?"

"Shoppers Mecca," he said, remembering the tree from his twelfth year. His mom shelled out for a Grow-Your-Own, the only way to get real trees then. It had been enormous, decorated with popcorn and ornaments generations old. The lights were miniature candles that appeared to be burning, and his parents had bought so many presents that the packages spilled across the living room floor.

"Was it fun?" She huddled in the chair, her legs drawn up to her chest, mug balanced on one knee.

He shrugged and thought. It had been so long since he had done the holiday thing. He was usually on some run or another, earning extra cash. "The anticipation was great," he said after a moment. "All month. The tree, the lights, the packages filled with surprises. The feeling that something magic could happen. That was fun."

She was staring at the stars, like he had, only her scarred features had a touch of wistfulness. "Never had any of that. The Shoppers Mecca or the religious stuff."

"Never? Not even as a kid?" He regretted the question the minute he asked it. She had spoken of her childhood enough—in the program from the age of 11, bounced at 16 when she became too hard to handle after her grand-mother's death, running freight ever since because she was strong and one of the best damn pilots in the business.

"Not the shopping. Not the religion." She finished her cocoa and set the mug on the floor beside her seat. "Christmas Eve, my Gram would fill a thermos with hot cocoa, then she would bundle me up, take me outside, and when we were all snug in the snow, drinking our cocoa, she'd point to the stars. She'd tell me this story about how, when she was a girl, they had this race to get to the moon, and how, one Christmas Eve, those astronauts orbited the moon for the first time, and they sent holiday wishes to Earth."

"Apollo 8," Hayes said. "Borman, Lovell, and Anders."

"You know it?" she asked.

"Space history is a hobby of mine."

She nodded, still staring at the blackness. "Anyway, Gram thought it was a miracle. A real miracle. So every year, she went outside and pretended she could see them up there, circling."

"So that's why you do this," Hayes said.

She looked at him for the first time, her nut-brown eyes bright. He could almost see the little girl, bundled against the cold, holding her grandmother's hand and staring at the night-darkened sky.

"No," she said, her flat voice shattering the illusion. "We were born too late to be cowboys, Hayes, and there's no such thing as miracles anymore."

She picked up her mug and straightened out her legs, then pushed out of the seat. Space was as dark as ever, the stars bright beacons of the future, waiting for him. But he would never go farther than Mars. He was a pilot who shuttled ore, equipment and people from place to place. Not even allowed the glamor title "astronaut" any more.

She had stopped behind his chair. He could see her reflection against the window as if she were standing in space, unsupported by the freighter.

"That's why I like this run on Christmas," she said. "I need to remember that once upon a time, this was the stuff of dreams."

She touched his shoulder, a fleeting warmth, a moment, dreamer to dreamer. Then she let go.

"More cocoa?" she asked.

"Yeah," he said, glad she had brought it along.

Before handing her his mug, he took one last sip. He stared at the stars, swirling the chocolate on his tongue, and savored the taste of miracles.

Stille Nacht

To the memory of my mother

THE GIRLS ARE FINALLY ASLEEP. I have waited until I hear no more giggles coming from the tiny bedroom. Now I have taken out the Santa presents, and they are scattered on the apartment's scarred hardwood floor. I sit in the narrow dining room, which gives me a good place to hide as well as a view of the hall.

It's hard to put the girls to bed on Christmas Eve. "Will Santa come, Mommy?" Suzanne asks me every year. "Will he really come?" And I know what she's asking. She's not asking about Santa. She's asking about Daddy.

"Santa will come, honey," I tell her and add silently, *Daddy won't.*

Gretchen, on the other hand, is simply aglow. She's too young to remember Will, too young to recall all the Christmases when Daddy said he would come and never did. The least I can do is make Santa reliable.

I dread the day when I tell Suzanne that Santa isn't real. That is, mercifully, a few years off, although she has heard rumors. Little Kevin Targe, whose parents believe in angels and don't believe in discipline, has told all the children that Santa is "a merchandising ploy designed to keep the masses happy." Fortunately, Suzanne doesn't understand "merchandising," "masses" or "ploy." She does understand "happy," and that's where I come in.

I hope.

Although, at the moment, I doubt it.

I am sitting in the middle of kitten and teddy bear wrapping paper, tape stuck to my upper arm (I'm too chicken to pull it off—I hate ripping the fine hairs), and am staring at Barbie's easy-to-assemble Malibu Beach House. I had one of those once, and it too arrived fully assembled under the tree.

I don't think I appreciated my own Santa until now.

I blow a strand of hair out of my face. I have dried cookie dough on my sweatshirt, and frosting beneath my nails. My butcher block table, purchased with hard-earned teaching dollars, has food coloring stains on its edges, child-size frosting prints on its surface, and red hots stuck to its legs. The dishes are in the sink, the kuchen dough chilling in the fridge, the remaining frosting is drying in its bowl. I have at least three more hours before I can sleep—that is, if Santa can assemble Barbie's Malibu Beach House without first getting an engineering degree. And the girls will wake me at the crack of dawn.

I am sipping Christmas tea from France, a fragrant blend made of black tea, caramel flavor, pineapple, and sweet oranges, my one indulgence this year. When I ordered it, I imagined myself in my immaculate kitchen, tree lights twinkling in the nearby living room, the girls asleep down the hall. At that moment, Christmas seemed like peace, like light, like warmth.

Like television.

I sigh, and flick on the radio. The local rock station is playing the Drifters' cover of "White Christmas," so I switch to public radio. The King's Singers, with promise of the Cambridge Boy's Choir later. Christmas carols, sung beautifully.

I stop and hold the tea. The mug, a Denny's holiday cup, is warm against my hands. My Christmases were beautiful as a little girl. Cookies, and kuchen, and carols. A house decorated in every room. And while Santa didn't always bring the right gifts, he brought gifts, drank his milk, and left a half-eaten cookie on the plate.

This is what I want for my girls: a moment of peace in a year filled with disappointments, with missing daddies, and macaroni and cheese suppers.

A moment of peace is all I ever wanted.

***

WE ALWAYS WENT TO CHURCH on Christmas Eve. Advent and Christmas are the only things I miss from my former religion: the smell of pine boughs and candles, the music sung with enthusiasm and love, and the sermon, always creative, always short. I got to stay up until midnight, and the world never looked more beautiful: white snow on the sidewalks, the hand-carved lanterns providing light into the church, the black sky above, the shouts of "Merry Christmas! Merry Christmas!" in the ice-coated air.

Mother insisted on church, just as she insisted on reading from Luke before we opened presents. She believed in keeping the Christ in Christmas long before the phrase was trendy, and it gave the holiday a mysticism that it seems to lack now. Sometimes I could almost feel the hope, and the magic, that the shepherds and the wise men felt as they gazed on the tiny baby, wrapped in swaddling clothes and lying in a manger.

Sometimes I almost believed.

***

"Mommy?" It is Suzanne. I bury the parts of Barbie's Malibu Beach House under a pile of wrapping paper, and slip into the hallway. It is dark and crowded despite the Mickey Mouse nightlight at the end. Apartment designers should remember that people have to live in these spaces.

"What, baby?" I whisper near her door, careful not to wake Gretchen.

"Has Santa come?" Her voice is tight with tension.

"Not yet, honey."

"He won't come when you're awake," she said.

I smile, and resolve to be even more quiet. "I'll go to bed soon."

"But what if we've already missed him?"

"We won't miss him, honey. Santa always comes."

"He didn't come to Katrina's house last year."

I sigh. How to explain why Santa misses the poor children in Suzanne's class? "I'm sure he tried," I say lamely.

"Mommy, what if he doesn't come?"

"He will, sweetie." I lean against her door jamb. She won't sleep anytime soon. "You want to get up and have some warm milk and honey? There's some pretty music on the radio."

"No, thanks," she says, sounding prim, sounding like my mother. "It's too late already."

***

I CAN STILL SEE HER, my mother, on all those Christmas Eves, her gray hair piled on the top of her head, her Christmas dress always green and red. She stands in the darkened pew beside me, holding a candle. The church lights are off, the candle is lit, illuminating her familiar face. She is singing "Silent Night"—only she refuses to sing it in English. She is a first generation American. Church to her should be conducted in German, and on Christmas Eve, singing the final hymn, she always rebels.

Stille Nacht. Heilige Nacht...

The memory fades there. I cannot remember the German words.

Or the sound of her voice.

***

BARBIE'S MALIBU BEACH HOUSE is finally assembled and under the tree. It looks perfect, even though I put the second floor where the ceiling should be. Gretchen's PlaySkool tree house stands beside it, easier to assemble and just as impressive.

Santa is tired.

And she still has kuchen to bake.

I sigh, go to the kitchen, and turn the radio on softly. The dough is firm. I take out my grandmother's rolling pin, and put down the baker's cloth. I melt butter in the microwave, sprinkle flour, and take out the dough.

My grandmother made this dough with her hands. My mother used a hand-beater. I use an electric mixer, one of the few wedding gifts that still works.

I flatten the kuchen, add cinnamon, sugar, and raisins, then roll dough into a tiny tube. I wind the tube into a pie plate, and clip the top with my mother's pastry scissors. She used to make the same movement, her fingers nimble and quick, not tired and stained like mine.

The kuchen is a link from generation to generation. My grandmother baked her kuchen in an oven heated by flame. My mother made it in a GE electric stove she bought with my father's life insurance money.

I use a tiny apartment stove whose temperature gauge no longer works.

***

MY GRANDPARENTS HAD NO MONEY. But my mother said they celebrated Christmas in style. My grandmother decorated every room in the house. She made all the presents, and baked for a month before. On Christmas morning, my grandfather opened the parlor and built a fire. When the room was warm, all nine children had to sit—one at a time—at the piano and sing a carol for my grandmother.

When they were finished, she took over the piano, and led them in a chorus of *Silent Night*.

In German.

***

THE KUCHEN IS BAKING and it finally smells like Christmas. I have had so much tea, my hands are shaking. The dishwater is a dirty lime green. Sprinkles float on top of it. I let the water drain, wipe my hands on the Santa towel I bought at Bi-Mart for ninety-five cents, and stare out the kitchen window.

The only lights in the neighborhood come from the decorations which everyone leaves on for Santa. Red and green and gold reflect in the snow. The night is dark.

And I am the only one awake.

Except for the disk jockey. He says he is playing one final King's Singers' carol before playing a rerun of Cambridge's Christmas service. It is already Christmas morning in England.

I put the stopper back in the sink and am about to fill it when the timer buzzes. I shut off the timer and open the stove. The kuchen is golden brown, the sugar melted, the raisins plump and juicy.

Heat caresses my face.

And then voices fill my kitchen.

Stille Nacht. Heilige Nacht…

The King's Singers are singing "Silent Night."

In German.

I take the kuchen out and set it on the cooling rack. I close the oven door, and listen.

The words are familiar and warm. This is how the carol should go.

But I cannot sing along. During all those years she stood beside me, all those years I listened to her high, fluted, and perfect soprano float over the congregation, I never bothered to learn the words.

I do not speak the language of her childhood.

I never have.

***

IT IS TWO HOURS BEFORE DAWN. I have just finished frosting the kuchen, just shut off the kitchen light, when I hear a creak in the hallway. I peer around the kitchen door to see my eldest daughter, her Garfield nightgown ghostly in the dimness of the night light, tiptoe into the living room.

She stops in front of the tree. Her hands rise to her mouth. She doesn't move for the longest time. Finally she crouches and touches Gretchen's tree house.

"He came," she whispers to the empty room. "He really came."

***

MY ROOM IS COOL, the bed inviting. I sink under the blankets and close my eyes, my body humming from tea, and sugar, and stress.

I am nearly asleep when I see my mother. Not singing in the candlelight, but as she looked on Christmas morning, her hair messed from sleep, a streak of flour on her cheek. She clutches a chipped mug of coffee in her right hand, and she has deep shadows beneath her eyes. She is watching me with an intensity I have never seen before, as if she could absorb my joy, my excitement into herself.

Then she sees me—the adult me.

Stille Nacht, she whispers.

Heilige Nacht, I whisper back.

We smile, and sleep finally comes.

Two hours of heavenly peace.

Afterword

WHEN I FINISHED PUTTING TOGETHER my short story collection, *Recovering Apollo 8 and Other Stories*, in 2009, I wrote about the genesis of the stories in the afterword. I didn't want to spoil the surprises for my readers, yet I wanted to talk about the stories themselves as honestly as I could.

Many readers told me that the afterward added a lot of fun to the collection. So I decided to follow the same format here.

I like to write stories filled with twists, so for heaven's sake, don't read this part of the book before reading the stories.

Warning: Spoilers Ahead.

***

Boz: "Boz" is the last story I wrote for our group Christmas readings. I had run out of time two nights before Christmas Eve, but wanted to have a story for the

Christmas party. I have no idea where the story came from, just that I sat down and started typing. I let Boz tell me the story, and the tale surprised even me.

Then Ellen Datlow picked it up for *SciFi.com*, surprising me even more. Although the critics ignored the story, it has remained a fan favorite ever since it was published.

***

Doubting Thomas: For years, my writing office overlooked Highway 101 going through Lincoln City, Oregon. I had a perfect view, not just of the ocean and the highway, but of a very popular store called the Christmas Cottage. On the roof of the Christmas Cottage are three Santas. One is sitting, one is climbing, and the other is looking at the chimney.

I guess, after years of wondering why there were *three* Santas instead of just one, something wormed its way into my brain. So when John Helfers asked me to write a story about a successful villain, I looked out my window and saw not one, not two, but three Santas.

And had my story.

***

Rehabilitation: The year I wrote this story, Oregon's largest newspaper, *The Oregonian*, did a feature on a man who had played a department store Santa for decades. From the time he was a young man and needed a fake beard to the day when he was old enough to grow his own. The entire center of this man's existence was the month of December. He even quit jobs so that he could play Santa.

It struck me—because I'm a mystery writer (and therefore a suspicious person) at heart—that no one ever checked his credentials. He simply got hired. Department stores let children sit on his lap, and he could be just anyone.

So of course, I found myself wondering what kind of anyone would want this job. And suddenly, I had a story. A mystery story. With a twist.

***

The Moorhead House: When I moved to Eugene, I found an apartment in one of the city's old neighborhoods. Dean, who did not live with me, found an apartment in the oldest building in the city, the Ankeny House. It was one of those lovely Victorians, with the suggestion of ghosts and a lot of history.

We had many adventures in that part of town, some of which will never get discussed. Many of our Christmas gatherings were held there.

Then, years later, after we had married and moved to the Oregon Coast, we drove past the Ankeny House and were surprised to see the entire place decked out for Christmas. I have no idea if someone had turned it back into a single-family dwelling or if the tenants had gotten together to decorate the house.

But it sat on a hill and looked both festive and eerie.

I had that image in mind when I started "The Moorhead House." The dark direction the story took has more to do with me than it does with beautiful old Victorian houses. Or maybe it was just the suggestion brought about by that brightly lit house on that dark hillside in the middle of a very foggy Christmas night.

***

Nutball Season: I must confess: "Nutball Season" is one of my favorite stories. I had fun writing it. I had even more fun reading it out loud for my friends. I also had fun publishing it, getting lots of letters after it appeared on *SciFi.com*. I have even read this story at science fiction conventions, if I attend the convention during the holiday season.

The idea didn't come to me in one piece. Just the voice. Nick Mantino was insistent. He wanted to tell me a story.

So I let him.

And have had fun with it ever since.

***

Loop: Honestly, I didn't remember this story until I started pulling out all of my holiday tales. Then I recalled where I wrote it, and when. Dean and I lived out in the country for a few years and held the Christmas gatherings there. By then, I was tired of writing ghost stories, and wanted to write something that counted, but wasn't a ghost story at all. So I wrote "Loop."

Dean liked it so much that he bought it for a computer magazine, *V.B. Tech Journal*. Dean was the fiction editor. He wouldn't let me send the story anywhere else.

After rereading it, I understand why he pulled it out of my hesitant fingers. Sometimes everything comes together, whether the writer knows it or not.

***

Substitutions: I have been writing about Silas, who deals in Death, since the early 1990s. In fact, I started "Substitutions" on December 20, 1996. I wrote the first three paragraphs and stopped, uncertain where the story was going to go.

Fast forward eight years. During that time, I would open the file, read my three paragraphs, and decide not to finish the story. Then Brittiany A. Koren asked me into an anthology she was editing with Martin H. Greenberg about assassins, called *Places to Be, People to Kill*. I realized at that moment that Silas could be considered an assassin. I opened the story again and this time, I finished it.

Soon after it was published, I received an email from Ed Gorman, a fine writer who edits an annual year's best mystery volume. He wanted "Substitutions" for his mystery anthology.

I was surprised. I hadn't thought of the story as a mystery. Once again, I learned that a story isn't what the writer thinks it is.

***

Snow Angels: For a while, Dean and I owned a Christmas tree farm. Actually, we bought the property for the view. We were going to build a house on top of the hill. We had 20 acres, most of it planted in Christmas trees. We thinned the crop, like you're supposed to do, and we let friends cut trees every year. Then we found our home on the Oregon Coast and sold the tree farm.

This story came quickly and it came from the experience of owning the tree farm. It was pretty isolated out there, and I had this feeling that anything could happen. So in this story, I made sure it did.

***

The Taste of Miracles: "The Taste of Miracles" was the first short story I wrote after I quit editing *The Magazine of Fantasy and Science Fiction*, and I was suffering from a problem that I call "critical brain." I finished the story, read it at our Christmas gathering, then decided it was "slight," and shelved it.

Years later, I found a copy, reread it, and loved it. It wouldn't win any awards, but it did exactly what I wanted it to do—it talked about an imagined future for outer space while harking back to the past. I immediately mailed the story to *Analog*, and Stanley Schmidt bought it just as fast. A lot of people write to me about this story, so I guess my judgment of the story was incorrect. It might be short, but readers like it.

***

Stille Nacht: Every Christmas I think of my mother. Christmas was her favorite holiday and she worked very hard to make the season meaningful. She was a minister's kid, the youngest in a very large family. Her father died at the age of 54. My mother was only eight. I think after that Christmas became an unpleasant holiday.

She bought me a Christmas ornament every single year, starting with my first Christmas, so that I would have enough ornaments to cover a tree when I moved away from home. I still have all of the ornaments and more. I also cook her recipes during the holiday.

We weren't close, but I feel close to her during December. I think that month she tried to achieve perfection, and more often than not, she came close.

She inspired this story. I just wish she'd lived long enough to see it in print. I suspect she would have loved it.

***

I HAVE A NUMBER OF HOLIDAY STORIES that haven't made it into this collection. Some can't be reprinted yet because of the contracts I signed. Some need to be scanned into my computer. The stories are so old I wrote them on an Apple //e and never converted the file.

So there will be more large Christmas collections. Maybe not next year, but the year after. Until then, individual stories will go up as electronic publications. And some stories will get scattered into five-story collections. I hope some day to edit a volume of the best stories from our Christmas Eve parties.

I have so many dreams and so little time.

Enjoy your time during the holiday season. I know I will.

About the Author

INTERNATIONAL BESTSELLING WRITER Kristine Kathryn Rusch has published fiction in every genre. She has been nominated for three Edgar Awards, two Shamus Awards, and an Anthony Award. She has won the *Ellery Queen* Reader's Choice Award twice. She has also won two Hugo awards, a World Fantasy Award, and three *Asimov's* Readers Choice Awards. She writes mystery as Kris Nelscott, paranormal romance as Kristine Grayson, as well as the science fiction and fantasy that she's known for under Rusch. For more information about her work, please go to kristinekathrynrusch.com.

Also by
Kristine Kathryn Rusch

The Retrieval Artist Series:

The Disappeared
Extremes
Consequences
Buried Deep
Paloma
Recovery Man
Duplicate Effort
Anniversary Day
Blowback

The Smokey Dalton Series (as Kris Nelscott):

A Dangerous Road
Smoke-Filled Rooms
Thin Walls
Stone Cribs
War at Home
Days of Rage

WMG
Publishing

www.ingramcontent.com/pod-product-compliance
Lightning Source LLC
Chambersburg PA
CBHW031952240626
47153CB00003B/956

* 9 7 8 0 6 1 5 7 3 3 6 3 0 *